Queer as Folk

by Celia Micklefield
(sometimes wearing her Mick Alec Idlelife head)

Copyright © 2017 Celia Micklefield
All rights reserved

ISBN: 13:978-1502955289

All characters and events in this publication are fictitious and any resemblance to real persons, living or dead, is purely coincidental

Cover photograph by Keighley News circa 1957

DEDICATION

Dedicated to my family and friends who understand that we are all queer as folk.

Where would we be without the people who matter in our lives with all their quirks and foibles?

Celia Micklefield 2017

This second collection of short stories has been a long time coming to fruition. There are a lot of reasons for that. One of those reasons lingers on and the author has learned to cope with it. Another reason has been got rid of and the author was glad to see the back of it.

Mick and Celia are happy they are in the position to be able to say - here it is - the second collection of short stories.

CONTENTS

Donors

What's for Dinner?

Lemon Meringue

Yorkshire Grit

January Girl

Like Mother, Like Daughter

The Fire Dragon

The Tenants

The Silent Movie Star

Tom's 2010 Cruise

What Time is it Mr Wolf?

Lost Dreams

14 Tweet Story

Airport Departures

Christmas Haunt

Resolution

Promises, Promises

A Gentle Message

Over the Hill

Blank Canvas

Far be it from Me

Spider Baby

A Practical Woman

Donors

The best thing to give your enemy is forgiveness; to an opponent, tolerance; to a friend, your heart; to your child, a good example; to a father, deference; to your mother, conduct that will make her proud of you; to yourself, respect; to all men, charity.

Francis Maitland Balfour 1851-1882

ONE

All sorts of people come to give blood. In my time when I worked on the blood collection circuits I'd dealt with all of them. I'm Denise. It was on my name badge. Not Nurse Middleton or anything respectful like that. No. Just Denise. As if we were operating a fast food outlet and I was going to serve you hamburger and fries. Management said first names made us look more approachable. Maybe management should have asked donors what *they* thought. If you ask me, most people actually prefer old-fashioned ways.

In some parts of the county there were women who turned up in twin sets and pearls. They smelled of powdery vanilla and lipstick and their shoes were made of softest leather that hardly made a sound when they walked. Must've cost a fortune. Their hairstyles were from a different era, swept back away from their faces and they said *Yah* instead of yes. The men smelled of spicy aftershave and fresh-washed cotton shirts. They wore their hair in sharp side partings. Their faces were clean shaved with outdoor cheeks. They looked a little conspicuous and slightly out of place as they parked their four by fours and stepped up to come inside.

Others came in their hacking jackets and green wellington boots and said they hadn't had time to wash the mud from their feet. They smelled of farmyards and animal feeds. After they made their donations they didn't like being cared for by the unit. They shrugged off efforts to encourage them to take the full recovery period. They called it *fuss* and didn't want plasters on their arms and fingers.

Yet there were many donors who looked as if their blood was all they had left to give. They wore shabby coats and their shoes were scuffed and down at heel. You might wonder how it is that people who have so little can still think of others less fortunate and want to help. I looked at them sometimes and wondered what it was that kept them coming. The *milk of human kindness*? Was it still out there? What special quality did these people have that made them rise above their own misfortunes? I don't know. Sometimes, I even forgot why it was I took to the job in the first place.

I was the oldest member of the mobile unit. We were the people who drive around the county and park outside supermarkets and in school playgrounds. We joked we were like community *vampires*, turning up every three or four months to suck people's blood. In a sense, it *is* sucked out. We had fat needles and tubes and special bags to store it in and if it wasn't for the blood collection units and people who come to donate there'd be many a chronically sick patient or emergency case who breathed their last for want of an *armful* of blood. That's another joke. I've lost count of the number of times I've heard that one.

I used to joke all the time.

"Look out. Here come the blue bloods," I'd say in one of the *horsey set* locations. "Mind your Ps and Qs."

And, "Never mind the blood bags. Where's the bloody biscuits?" I'd say before we opened up the doors. I'd make up nicknames too for the regular donors, never unkind and never in front of their faces but funny all the same.

It grew hard to keep up with the joking. Sometimes I'd catch myself complaining again about long hours and awkward customers. I disappointed myself. I knew I sounded like a misery but I didn't seem able to stop. It was as if my heart got too heavy for light-heartedness; my tongue got too sour to make jokes.

"Oh, get me a gun," I'd say at half an hour to closing when there was still a queue outside, "and I'll shoot the bloody lot of 'em." And then I'd laugh but it made an uncomfortable sound like fingernails on a blackboard. The others pulled sympathetic faces. I knew they worried about me.

The others: Alan, he was the session nurse. His role was a bit like the supervisor of the team. There was Stuart who used to be a paramedic until he hurt his back; Molly, who didn't want to go back into full-time nursing after she had her children and Kirsty who at twenty one was still a novice. That was my unit. They were my people.

We covered a lot of ground: all over the county and beyond, big city centres and country villages where there was no village hall. There are different teams who go out to places where there's a suitable indoor venue. They take racks and crates of stuff with them and have to move it all in and out again but we had everything we needed to hand except for proper beds. Our donors sat in specially moulded seating where they could get their legs above their heads in case of fainting and we could deal with only three donors at a time while another two filled in their questionnaires.

It got crowded inside the van. That's something else that annoyed me especially in summer when on hot days it was so stuffy. Inside metal walls with the sun beating down on the roof, the air sometimes felt too thick to breathe. And, of course, there were all those packages of life-saving blood sitting in their containers like little hot water bottles. New donors were often surprised by the warmth radiating from those soft, plastic bags. We could get a bit smelly too sometimes with the number of bodies in such a hot, small space, the headiness of the team's countless alcohol wipes and the whiff of nervous perspiration from first time donors.

"Never mind, Denise," Molly used to say. "Not long to go now, eh? When you've retired, you'll be able to stay in bed in the mornings."

"And you'll be at home to eat dinner at the same time as your husband," Stuart might add.

Somehow though, it didn't help when they told me how chilled my life would be when I retired. They didn't know how anxious I was about losing my work. I suppose that's *why* I did so much grumbling. I was pretending I hated the job. I didn't know what I'd call myself when I stopped working. I felt it would be as if I would lose any *worth*. I tried not to think about it. I stifled a sigh when I felt one rising at the back of my throat but it always worked its way out down my neck and along my arms. It tingled through my hands and flicked at my fingers. When it was my turn to drive the van I'd feel it when I changed gear, always hurried, always as if my hands were angry.

"Slow down, Denise," Alan would say. "It's not the Monaco Grand Prix."

"The sooner we get there, the sooner we can pack up and go home," I'd tell him but we all knew that wasn't true because we had to stay right till the end of the shift whether or not people came. But I rushed through city streets or along country lanes as if I wanted to hasten the end of the day, the end of the week, the month, the year, to hurry along that final day at work and get the pain of it over and done with.

Alan knew to the centimetre how wide we were, the best places to park, and he always had something to say when one of us took the wheel.

"Park it facing downhill," he joked when it was Stuart's turn, "It'll make the blood come out faster."

Molly didn't drive but Kirsty took a turn just the once. Alan watched her like a hawk waiting to dive on its supper.

"Change down, change down, first gear now round this sharp corner, hold it on the clutch. Look out! Mind that bollard."

"Can't you see you're making her nervous?" Molly said.

"Keep your eyes on the road,"Alan shouted and he didn't see how Kirsty's mouth trembled and her eyes filled with tears.

"Look out!" he shouted again. I leaned over and gave him a shove.

"Leave her alone, Alan. You're a right pain."

"Well, you'll be rid of me soon, won't you when you're a lady of leisure?"

"I can't wait."

Alan didn't approve of how Kirsty had parked and insisted she moved aside to let him put us somewhere else. She wouldn't drive again after that.

We were outside the council offices one Monday morning. *Moonface* was the first appointment. He was only nineteen. He had huge round eyes staring up out of his big face. The first time he came to give blood he was nervous and shy. Then he became more confident but his eyes still followed his carer like they were stuck. He *loved* all the attention and the questions and form-filling and plasters and tea and biscuits afterwards.

"Hello," Molly said as she greeted him. "Nice to see you again. You've got me again today. Is that all right with you, Paul?"

And we all knew it was perfectly all right with Paul Moonface to have Molly looking after him. We could tell by his *moony* eyes and that satisfied grin in his round face.

Bob came in next: he was another regular from the council offices. He always smelled of pipe tobacco and mints. His pipe was sticking up out of the breast pocket of his jacket.

"When are you going to quit that dirty habit?" Alan said. "Your blood's getting so full of nicotine it takes twice as long to filter."

"You're still glad to have it, though," Bob retaliated and the jokes began again. "Anyway," Bob went on, "I don't believe you. I only have two pipes full a day. One after lunch, here, outside in the smokers' shed and one at home after my evening meal. If I didn't have my evening pipe to look forward to I'd die of stress."

"Stress?" Alan said. "You call working for the council stress? You want to come out with us for a day, Bob. We'll show you what stress is all about."

"My granddad used to smoke a pipe," Kirsty said. "I liked that smell when I was little. Now, it always reminds me of Christmas. It goes with the smell of pine and cinnamon. You know, a *Christmassy* smell."

"Why did he stop?" Bob asked.

Kirsty said, "Stop what?"

"Why did he stop smoking a pipe? You said he *used* to."

"Oh, well, he didn't really stop," she said. "He died."

"Good enough reason, I suppose," Bob said and Kirsty blushed.

"Oh," she said. "That's not what I meant, Mr Armitage. Oh dear, I'm sorry. No, it wasn't the pipe smoking that killed him. He fell off a bus and banged his head."

Kirsty's last remark pretty much killed that conversation and everybody went quiet for a while.

Paul Moonface finished his session and the lady from IT came in. Bob finished and said he'd be back again in three months if he hadn't fallen off the mortal coil before then. The rest of the booked appointments took us to lunchtime.

Lunch was always a hurried affair. It was a case of grab what you can when you can because if a member of the public turned up unexpectedly without an appointment, we didn't turn them away. We managed somehow.

I think the majority of the general public don't realise the short shelf life of blood products so we never turned people away without good reason. Sometimes we had to but it was never because it was lunchtime. It might be because they were underweight or they had a cold or because their iron count was low. That doesn't mean they could *never* be a donor. We explained that a sick person needs best quality blood to help them get better. And, we wouldn't want to make future donors feel unwell by taking from someone whose iron was low, for example, and put them off coming back.

So it felt like any other ordinary day at the blood collecting session outside the council offices. The cherry blossom trees were at their May best, branches burgeoning with heavy, pink blooms. Above, clouds like white marshmallows washed across the sky so that everything looked clean and fresh. In the council flowerbeds anemones nodded their colourful faces in the breeze; snapdragons bobbed between: a perfect day for the end of spring carrying all the promise of summer.

The afternoon appointments began and the seats were filling up when there was a knocking on the side of the van although the door was standing open.

"You can come right in," Alan called, looking up from where he was occupied with another donor.

A man came in. He was tall and he stood straight with his chin held up. His hair was cut very short, clipped extra short at the neck. He wore a long-sleeved sweatshirt even though the day was pleasantly warm. Beneath his cargo pants his trainers looked so white and clean they must have been brand new. They hadn't seen much rain or mud.

"Yay! A *Newbie*," Stuart said. "Sir, you are very welcome."

"Please, take that seat by the door," Alan said, "We'll be with you in a minute. Kirsty? You're free now, aren't you?"

The man sat. He kept his back as stiff and upright as when he was standing up. His legs were tight and tense and he tapped out a rhythm with his heels as if he was on starting blocks in a race, on the point of thrusting upwards and running out again. His eyes were so intense they looked fierce and they darted all around the interior of the van and kept flicking back toward the entrance.

Kirsty handed him the New/Returning Donor form and explained what was required. His eyes lost some of that ferocity and he looked at the floor.

"I'll need some help with that," he said.

"Would you like me to read it for you?" Kirsty said.

"No. I can read it. I can't fill it in."

"I've got a pen for you here," Kirsty said and held it out.

"You don't understand," the man said. "Writing is a problem for me just now."

"No problem," Kirsty said with that wide young person's smile of hers. "Shall we do it together?"

"I'd prefer it if you got rid of that patronising tone of voice," the man said.

"Oh, I'm sorry. I didn't mean . . ." Kirsty began.

"Look. Let's just get on with it."

Stuart looked away. Molly and I were occupied but Alan was nearly finished.

"Would you like me to take over, Kirsty?" he asked.

"There's no need for that," the man said. "She's capable of ticking a few boxes, isn't she? Even if I'm not."

They began with his name. Alex Scott. He hesitated over 'Title'. It seemed to take him overlong to pronounce the word *Mister*. He was thirty four but looked older especially around those suspicious grey eyes where sun exposure had burned lines into his skin. The *lifestyle* questions made him smirk.

"I'm sorry," Kirsty apologised again, "but we have to ask these questions about sexual activity. We have to ask everybody, every time they come. It's part of the job."

Behind her where I was finishing with some paperwork, I smiled. We all knew how long it had taken Kirsty to overcome her embarrassment at some of the lifestyle questions.

His general health was good, he affirmed. No recent viruses. No coughs and colds. He wasn't on any medication. He'd had no recent tattoos. The one on his shoulder, underneath his thick sweater, he'd had since he was eighteen, he said.

Kirsty moved on to the questions in the next section.

"In the last twelve months have you been outside the UK?" she asked.

"Yes."

Kirsty ticked the box.

"Have you ever stayed outside the UK for a continuous period of six months or more?" she asked.

"Yes."

"Oh," she said. "You've lived abroad? Was it somewhere nice?"

His eyes grew fierce again. His mouth drew into a thin, tight line.

"Afghanistan," he said.

"Oh? On business?"

"You could say that. Government business."

He seemed reluctant to say more. Alan coughed and tried to attract Kirsty's attention.

"I've seen it on the news," Kirsty went on. "It's a dangerous place to go on business. All those bombings and everything. Weren't you afraid?"

He laughed, a guttural sound, like a cracked bell.

"*Everybody's* afraid out there," he said. "Some people are even afraid of their own shadows. Their own family. Their own children."

Kirsty said, "How awful."

"You get used to it."

Alan intervened.

"I think Mister Scott might have been in the military, Kirsty."

"You're a soldier?" she said. "You're a soldier?"

"*Was* a soldier. Sergeant. Not any more."

"Didn't you like it?"

"Yes, I liked it. I liked it a lot. It liked me. In the beginning. We had cocktails at six every evening and party nights with dancing girls."

"You didn't," Kirsty said, her eyes all wide with wonder.

"You'll be asking me next if I ever killed anybody," Alex Scott said, his eyes scrunched narrow and ferocious. He was sitting bolt upright in his seat, looking like a wild animal ready to pounce. Kirsty bit her lip and looked abashed. Her cheeks flushed. Alex continued his attack. "You wouldn't ask a waiter if he'd ever served plates of food, would you? You wouldn't ask a teacher if . . ."

I excused myself from my donor and stepped across the van to where Alex was sitting. I leaned in and kept my voice low.

"Mister Scott," I said. "Alex. Kirsty didn't actually ask you that question. Carry on, Kirsty. Sample next as usual." I went back to my place.

Kirsty took a deep breath and explained the reasons for the sample taken from the finger and the tests she would carry out immediately before they proceeded.

"Which arm would you like me to use?" she said, avoiding looking at him directly.

With his left hand Alex Scott held out an empty right sleeve and jiggled it in front of Kirsty's face.

He said, "I don't have a choice, do I?" Kirsty's mouth dropped open. Her eyes immediately filled. "That's why I can't fill in your bloody forms," he said. "That's why I'm not fit for a soldier now."

"I'm so, so, sorry," Kirsty said. She dropped the questionnaire, ran down the steps of the mobile unit and out into the council car park. She threw herself on the grass beneath one of the cherry trees, leaning back against the trunk, her shoulders heaving. Then she curled into a ball and hugged her knees.

Alex Scott got up to leave.

"Not giving a donation today?" I called across to him. "Never mind. Kirsty is still in her training period, Mister Scott. Thank you for providing her with some first- hand experience of dealing with a difficult situation. I'm sure she'll appreciate it."

Alex Scott stiffened his shoulders and jutted his chin. For a moment it looked as if he was going to say something. Briefly, his eyes softened and his jaw relaxed. Then, he turned on his heels and stepped outside. He looked over at where Kirsty was sobbing beneath the cherry tree. She was still in a tight ball, her head on her knees. He stood rigid, his mouth drawn tight, his eyes vacant. He turned his back on her and strode away into the spring afternoon, his bright, white shoes scything the air at his feet, his empty sleeve fallen loose and flapping in the sunshine.

TWO

Alex Scott's outburst had affected everybody including the donors we were attending. We fell silent. It was a strange kind of prickly silence. Kirsty was outside. Through the van's open door I could see her weeping under the cherry tree but inside the mobile unit it was as if the air had been completely sucked out leaving us in a vacuum, struggling to breathe. We were like fish, newly netted, mouths agape. Nobody knew what to say; I think nobody wanted to be first to speak.

It was as if Alex Scott had come, not out of the milk of human kindness thinking about doing something for other people, but to cause trouble. Right from the start, it seemed to me, he'd been awkward, difficult to deal with. I knew he must have experienced ghastly horrors beyond imagination during his service in Afghanistan. You heard tales about things nobody would want to see. And some of those lads in the military, well, they were just boys, weren't they? Some of them were not emotionally equipped to deal with the horrors of war.

Alex Scott wasn't a young kid, though. He'd lost his arm in the service of his country and then because of that he'd lost his military career but he'd made no attempt to be reasonable in his dealings with Kirsty. He wasn't the only person injured in service. He didn't have to be so nasty.

We would have to fill in a report when there was time. Whenever we had a little incident we filled out a report. We had to be sure of where we stood in case somebody made a complaint against us. As far as I was concerned, though, Kirsty had done nothing wrong.

As soon as I'd finished with my donor and given her a cup of tea, I slipped out. The others carried on with their work. Outside, I lowered onto the ground beside Kirsty. It took me a while. My hips weren't as young as they used to be. I struggled to get comfortable, sweeping away gravel and adjusting the waistband on my work trousers so they didn't fall down with me. My knees cracked as I shuffled about. Kirsty raised her head. She sniffed.

"You shouldn't be out here, Denise. The grass is still a bit damp," she said. Her voice was like a little girl's, shivery and breathless.

"Well that's a bugger," I said. "I'll never get back up now I've got all the way down here. I'll just have to stay where I am and get a wet backside."

We sat quietly for a while. I passed a tissue to Kirsty and she wiped her eyes and blew her nose.

"I'm sorry, Denise," she said, after a moment. "I've made a fool of myself, haven't I?"

"Not at all," I said. "Don't you worry about that, my love. The man was out of order."

"I should have noticed he didn't have a right arm."

"None of us noticed, Kirsty. Not the way he was sitting, sideways on like that like he was hiding it, keeping that side of him away from us. We were all so busy. How could any one have seen?"

"He must have felt awful."

"Not a good enough reason to make everybody else feel awful."

I watched her attempting to take control of her feelings. She swallowed and blew her nose again and for a moment it looked as if all might be well. But, it was too much for her. Her emotions were too raw. She collapsed into fits of sobbing again and I knew she was thinking about her brother.

"Kirsty," I said. "Would you like me to speak to Alan? I think you should go home."

"Oh, no," she said. "I can't do that. What would the others think?"

"Sweetheart. Don't you think you came back to work a little too soon? Hmmm? It takes a long time to come to terms with a bereavement. I bet you haven't been sleeping properly, have you?"

She shook her head.

"I thought not. Kirsty, you're exhausted. Take a few days off."

I rolled over onto my knees and pushed myself up to a crouching position before I could get up properly and stand beside her. Kirsty got up too.

"I'll finish the shift," she said, "but I will take some time off. You're right. I need to rest."

"You promise?"

She nodded. Poor Kirsty. Life hadn't been easy for her. Only twenty one and already there'd been so much tragedy in her young life. I don't understand how it is the nicest people sometimes get such a raw deal when villains and scoundrels seem to sail through life without a moment's worry. There's no wonder you can get cynical as you grow older. That's my excuse, anyway.

We walked back to the van. Kirsty went in first.

"I'm so sorry, everybody," she said.

"Apology accepted,'"Alan said. He didn't even look up from what he was doing. He didn't see Kirsty's face, reddened and puffy with dark rings under her eyes.

Men, I thought. I couldn't just stand there and say nothing.

"Alan," I said. "Kirsty needs some time off. Don't you, dear?"

"Ah," he said. "Well, I suppose we could rearrange your shifts .. ."

"Never mind about that just now. Kirsty doesn't need to know the details right this minute, Alan."

He looked as if he was going to start arguing but I threw him a look and he understood. He nodded and managed a comforting smile. "Take the rest of the week off," he said to Kirsty. "If you need more time you'll need a doctor's note."

Kirsty worked through the rest of the afternoon. She still looked tired and she'd lost her usual bright enthusiasm but she perked up a little when Bizzy came in. Bizzy's real name is Lizzie. Kirsty and she were schoolmates. She was a fussy little thing, always fidgeting, always talking. *Bizzy buzz. Bizzy buzz.* Kirsty liked the rapid repartee and usually gave as good as she got but I found it annoying, like wasps at a picnic. Bizzy came speeding up the steps out of breath.

"Am I late? Am I late? If I'm late I'm so sorry. Sorry Kirsty. Sorry everybody. Only, you'll never believe what just happened. . ."

"What?" Kirsty said.

"Take a seat, Lizzie," I said. "And calm down, dear. Hmmm? Just take a minute, please. You sound a bit over excited. We don't want you passing out on us, now do we?"

Bizzy flopped onto a seat and kicked off her shoes. Huge wedges, they were. It must have felt like walking on stilts. They wouldn't have passed a health and safety assessment, shoes like that. She reached in her bag for her mobile phone and began texting immediately.

What is it about youngsters today? Why must they always be on their phones? If it isn't a phone it's a tablet or whatever they call them. Texting here; messaging there. What's wrong with actually acknowledging the people you're with?

"Kirsty, why don't you take care of your friend, today?" I said, and to Bizzy added, "and you'll need to put away your phone, please. Thank you."

"Okay," she said. "No problem."

She scrunched her nose.

"You should have seen it, Kirsty," she said. "I couldn't believe it."

She still had the phone in her hand. She was showing Kirsty a photo she'd taken with it. She saw me shaking my head and tutting. "I won't be a minute," she said to me. "Honest."

"Oh!" Kirsty said, looking at Bizzy's phone. "It's him. Denise, look!"

I leaned over Kirsty's shoulder to take a look at Bizzy's photograph. There was a picture of Alex Scott. He was climbing down from a tree holding a kitten in his teeth.

"He climbed up to save it," Bizzy Lizzie said. "There was this enormous crowd standing watching him. Well, a crowd anyway. This little kitten had got stuck and this feller just shinned up the tree and fetched it back down, *in his teeth* just like a mother cat would do and then he gave it to this little girl who was crying her eyes out and then this feller, him here, just walked away and the funny thing about it was, when I got a good look at him, the man only had . . ."

"One arm," Kirsty and I said together.

"Yeh, right," Bizzy said, her mouth slack with surprise. "How did you know I was going to say that?"

"We've seen him before," I said.

Bizzy switched off her phone and put it away.

"Well, *I* thought it was strange," she said. She seemed disappointed we'd spoiled her punchline. "Tell me this, then. How could he climb a tree with only one arm?"

"He was probably very fit," I said.

"Well nobody else was offering to go up there," Bizzy said. "I thought he was very brave."

"I'm sure he is," I said.

Bizzy grabbed the phone from her bag again.

"I took a video clip of him climbing back down. Do you want to see it?"

"No. That won't be necessary," I said. "We believe you."

I glanced at Kirsty. She was okay keeping up the chatter with her old schoolfriend. I left Kirsty to get on and carried on with my own work but I couldn't stop thinking about Alex Scott.

I could see his sun-burned face and suspicious grey eyes, lines etched into the skin around them. I recalled the way he was on edge, watching everything around him, those eyes always on the move, scanning, searching, checking the exit, his body at the ready. Ready for what? What a complicated man he must be. A tortured soul, perhaps. Like many returning war veterans. Troubled. Unwell. Too proud to seek help, I guessed.

We worked far into the evening. It was after nine by the time we returned to base to park the van. Twilight was deepening into night. Rain clouds were gathering, darkening the sky. The air was chilly, the wind coming in from the east. I was glad of my jacket.

I usually gave Kirsty a lift home; it wasn't too far out of my way. She turned up the collar on her coat and tucked her scarf into it. Where earlier in the day her face had been reddened from crying, now her skin was so pale it looked grey. She was worn out, poor thing. She flopped into the front passenger seat. The seat covers were clammy and cold, a shock against my back and legs. I put the heater on full.

"I don't know what I'm going to do without you when you leave work, Denise," Kirsty said as I pulled out of the parking lot.

"I'm not going to Australia, Kirsty," I told her. "I'll still be here. You know where I live and you've got my number."

She smiled and nodded.

"I know. Thank you," she said.

She could hardly speak she was so tired. I could see she was on the point of falling asleep. Her eyelids were drooping and her head flopped to the side against the passenger window.

My own eyes ached. I'm not good at night driving; I find it such a strain, especially after a long day at work. Night had closed in. A car was following too close and its headlights reflecting in my rear view mirror were making me scrunch up my eyes, giving me a headache. I tried to ignore them. Each time I had to slow for traffic or make a turn the headlights behind me almost blinded me. I was feeling exhausted as I dropped Kirsty off by her block where she lived in the apartment she used to share with her brother. It would still feel strange for her, having to go home to an empty house. A car pulled up in the street behind me. Strong lights flashed in my mirrors. For a moment I could hardly see a thing. I was glad when its lights went off.

"Are you sure you'll be all right tonight?" I said.

"Yes, thank you. I'm going to make some hot chocolate and then go straight to bed," Kirsty said.

"Have some toast as well. You haven't eaten much today."

"Yes, Mum."

"Get away with you."

"I'll text you tomorrow."

"Good. Don't forget or I'll be round here knocking on the door to see how you are."

She went indoors. I waited until I saw the lights go on in her living room two floors up and she came to the window to pull on the curtains. She waved good night and I tooted the horn as usual. I pulled away from the kerb. Rain began to fall. Headlights came on again behind me. I tried not to look at them.

"Damnation," I muttered as bright white headlights followed me away from Kirsty's estate. Those brilliant white lamps are the worst ones. If you ask me, they should be banned. I've often thought they were dangerous. What's the matter with the ones we've always had? Who said we had to change them? Yellowish light is much better. You can see where you're going without blinding everybody coming the other way. Or the person in front of you.

I turned out of the estate toward the town centre. Rain continued. The road surface was soon shiny and slick. Out onto the main road, the startling headlights were still behind me. At the traffic lights along the High Street I had to stop. Angrily, I stared through my rear view mirror trying to make out the offending driver, not that I would have been able to do anything, but all I could see was shadow and wet reflections on the road surface.

We moved off again. I thought the car might overtake me once we'd left the built-up area but no, there it was still, following too close. Beyond the town the tree-lined road runs by open farmland. It's a pretty run during daylight when sunlight filtering through the tree canopy casts dappled shade on the road. At night it looks completely different. There are no street lights. It's very dark. Tree trunks slide past in the blackness. They appear dangerously near. The good thing is, you can easily see when a vehicle is coming the other way; you can see their lights from a long way off. I thought, *now he'll go past*. I slowed and moved as far to the left as I could to give the car behind space and opportunity to overtake.

"Come on, then," I shouted at the driver behind as if he or she would be able to hear. "What are you waiting for? Get past."

No joy. I crawled along as close to the line of trees as I dared. I was so close to them I could make out the patterns of tree bark as I glanced sideways, concentrating fiercely on steering a straight path with those damned lights in my eyes. The car sat behind me as if it were stuck.

"Go past," I screamed at my rear view mirror. "Can't you see I've slowed down to let you go?"

I speeded up again as the road straightened out, anxious now to get home. I wanted to get off the road. I wanted to get away from the annoying driver behind me. I needed to reach the comfort of my home. I imagined rushing indoors, slamming the door behind me and shutting out the night.

Ian would be watching for me. He'd be standing by the window, peering round the curtains ready to put on the kettle as soon as he saw me reversing into the drive. I'd dash upstairs and get out of my uniform. Wash my hands. Then, he'd retrieve my plate from the oven and I'd sit to eat. It would be Shepherd's Pie. In my imagination I could smell it already. Ian makes a good Shepherd's Pie. My stomach rumbled and I realised my mouth was actually watering.

Those little rituals of my daily homecoming suddenly felt so precious. At that moment with the strain of driving home in the wet and the dark with fierce headlights scorching my eyes, the comfort of those everyday things was all I wanted. Later, Ian and I would talk about other things but first he would wait till I had unwound. He would pour me another cup of tea and wait until I was ready to talk. He knows me so well.

Lights in the middle of the road. Not lights. What the . . .? Eyes! I don't want to hit it.

I swerved off to my right to avoid the fox in the road. My rear wheels began to slip and the car skated into a glide. I remember thinking,

What do I do now?
Turn into the skid.

I turned the wheel. Those headlights were still behind me. Bright and white and infuriating. Was that idiot of a driver watching me? I was conscious of feeling angry, not afraid. I wasn't fearful of an impending accident in the car; I was still furious with the driver behind me. I felt a shift in the direction of the slide and my tyres gripped the road again. I was able to right the car.

I realised I'd been holding my breath. I let it go. I slowed again. The car behind me slowed. I considered pulling up and stopping. What would he do then? A prickling sensation on the back of my neck made me shiver. There was no other traffic. Nobody to witness whatever might happen. I decided against. I kept going. The car continued to follow.

My pulse quickened. That car following me was no coincidence. It was deliberate. The driver was purposely tailing me, slowing when I slowed. Was that the same car that pulled up behind me when I dropped Kirsty at her flat? Had he been following me all this way?

I reached for my mobile to call Ian but in the darkness couldn't read the screen or find the right button. I wanted to ask my husband to come to the end of the drive but I'd never learned how to do the rapid dial thing. I couldn't use the phone without stopping and putting on the interior light. I'd need my reading glasses too. I was afraid to stop. Even with all the car doors firmly locked I would be vulnerable out on the road by myself. I had to get home.

Ten more minutes passed. The car was still behind me. I skirted around the leisure centre car park near our estate. I felt marginally better because there were plenty of street lights now and other cars and people. I turned the corner too fast. Tyres screeched and I almost lost control. I saw the lights outside our front door and the shape of my husband standing at the window. I wanted to weep with relief.

Instead of reversing as usual I drove straight into our drive. I stopped, pulled on the handbrake, leaned on the horn and kept my arm there, pressing with all my weight. The front door opened and cast light along our garden. I heard Ian running down the path to get me.

"Denise. Denise," he was shouting. "What's happened? I'm here. Open the door."

I opened the car door and got out. Ian grabbed me before I fell. "Look at you," Ian said. "Denise. You're in a state. What's the matter? What's been going on?"

"I've been followed," I told my husband, gasping, fighting back tears. "Someone's been following me in their car."

"I'm really very sorry about that," a voice said. "I meant no harm. I just wanted to talk to you."

A tall man stood under the lamppost. His back was straight and stiff. His grey eyes were troubled. Alex Scott.

THREE

"You wanted to what?" I screamed. "You wanted to *talk* to me? Have you any idea what you have just put me through?"

I knew I was screeching like a banshee, my voice soaring up to top pitch, my arms flailing around at my sides. I was beside myself, raving, angry with this man who, after annoying me with his damned infuriating headlights had then filled me with fear for my life. I was crazed with the relief of finding myself safe after all. Through my tirade Alex Scott simply stood there under the street lamp in the rain, his short hair spiky and wet, his head lowered like a puppy who knows he's done wrong.

"Are you all right?" he asked me. "I saw you get into that skid."

"Denise, who is this man?" Ian said. "What skid? And why are we standing out here in the rain?"

I was too emotional to answer. Fear had dissolved away into fury. I wanted to carry on screaming at Alex Scott for scaring the living daylights out of me. If he'd come any closer, I might have hit him. The three of us stood like statues on the gravel drive outside our house letting the rain soak us, each waiting for the others to speak.

"Come on," Ian said eventually. "We'd better go inside. You too, mate."

"No. I think it would be better if I just left you alone,'"Alex said and turned to walk away.

"Don't you dare," Ian called after him. "You owe me an explanation. You're not going anywhere till you tell me why you were following my wife."

Ian ushered me into the house. Alex Scott trooped after us. The kitchen smelled of my warmed-up dinner but I'd lost my appetite. My head was spinning. Ian poured tea and I took a cup. Alex refused at first.

"Get a bloody cup of tea, man," Ian said to him. "You can use that left hand of yours, can't you? You're wet through. I'll get you a towel." He looked at me then. "Denise," he said, "go and get out of those wet clothes. Go on, love. Me and our friend here will get acquainted."

I went to the bathroom. I dropped my uniform into the linen basket and looked for something to put on. Normally, I would have thrown on PJs and a comfortable dressing gown on top. Not tonight. I had a feeling Ian and Alex's talk could go on for some time. I knew they had a lot in common. I could hear them talking as I came down.

"Falklands.Two Para," Ian was saying.

"Afghan. 42 Commando, Royal Marines," I heard Alex Scott reply.

What is it about ex-Squaddies that they can recognise each other out of uniform, out of service, even when they've never met before?

"Ten years they've been killing our guys out there," Alex said.

They stopped talking as I entered the kitchen. Alex jumped to his feet.

"I apologise to you, Ma'am. For that business out there on the road. Sincerely. It didn't occur to me I was scaring you."

He looked so contrite, I softened. And that *ma'am* made me feel like royalty.

"You didn't scare me at first," I told him. "I was angry to begin with. It's those bright white headlights on your car. Then I got frightened when you wouldn't overtake. I thought I was being followed by . . . well, anyway, you know."

"So, you'd already met my wife?" Ian said.

"Yes. I went to give blood this afternoon." He looked at me and shrugged. "But it didn't work out."

"Is that why you wanted to talk to Denise?" Ian said.

"Yes."

"It wasn't me you were rude to," I said. "There's somebody else who deserves an apology."

"Is somebody going to tell me exactly what's been going on?" Ian said, "and do you mind if we eat while you're telling me?"

I said, "Haven't you had yours?"

"No. I decided to wait for you tonight." Ian pulled open the oven door and lifted out the dish of Shepherd's Pie. Its aroma filled the kitchen and immediately my appetite returned.

"I'll leave you to it," Alex Scott said and turned toward the door.

"Have you eaten?" Ian said to him. "There's enough here for three."

"Thank you, but I think I've caused enough trouble today without taking your dinner as well."

"Take a bloody seat, man. When was the last time you had a pie like this?"

Ian set it on the table. Alex Scott smiled at it.

"It looks damned good," he said.

He didn't take much more persuading. Ian won him over. He stayed to eat with us.

"So, Alex," Ian said after a few minutes. "Why *were* you following Denise?"

"I wanted to apologise for the way I went off on one at the blood collecting session but I didn't want to follow the young girl," Alex said. He looked at me. "I was there behind you when you dropped her off but something told me it wouldn't be a wise move to go knocking on her door."

"You're right. It wouldn't," I said.

"Look, I know I was out of order but I don't understand why she got so upset."

"Are we talking about young Kirsty?" Ian said.

"Yes. It was Kirsty who acted as carer for Alex. You know I can't talk about this, Ian. Patient confidentiality."

"What patient? He's here, isn't he? He wants to talk about it. Don't you?"

"Well, Kirsty isn't here to speak for herself," I said. "All I can tell Alex is she's had a very difficult time lately."

"And you, Alex?" Ian said. "You have family?"

Alex laid down his knife and fork and took a moment.

"I do," he said. "Yes. I have family. Not here though. My parents live in Cyprus and my sister went out there too with her husband and kids."

"Cyprus?" I said. "How lovely to live in permanent summer."

"Nah. It's not for me. I'm not a beach and sunshine sort."

"No wife and kids of your own?" Ian asked.

You'd think Ian was being nosey. Anybody else would naturally jump to that conclusion. But I know my husband. He doesn't do or say anything without a purpose. As soon as I heard them earlier exchanging names of regiments and places where they'd seen action, I knew where Ian would lead the conversation.

"I had a wife," Alex said. "But she left. Ran off with some bloke who had a safer job. Better prospects. Fortunately, we had no kids."

"So you live on your own?"

"I rent a place. Yes."

"Not found employment yet?"

"I'm working on it. Bloody good pie this."

"Don't change the subject. I know it's a bloody good pie. I made it. What kind of work would you like to get into?"

"I haven't really thought it through yet."

"Maybe you should."

"Did you?"

"Did I what?"

"Get work as soon as you came home from the Falklands?"

"Like some more pie, Alex?"

"Don't change the subject."

I listened to them bouncing off one another. I saw how Alex relaxed in Ian's company. He was leaning back against his chair, those grey eyes of his softer than I'd seen them. I noticed how Ian grew more animated. It had been a long time since he'd come across another 'old' soldier. I knew it wouldn't be long before they'd start trading action stories, comparing experiences.

Over the years I've seen how Ian returns to the subject of the Falklands war and each time it seems to me he is unburdening. He always talks about how he never expected to have to fight; how the lads thought by the time the troops sailed that far the problems would have been sorted out over some diplomatic table. He was due to come out of the military and had started planning a future in Civvy Street. He stayed on for that one last adventure. That's what he thought it was going to be: an adventure.

Alex Scott knew what *he* was going into. And I knew by the expression on his face he was ready to talk about it. I'd seen Ian wear that expression so many times when the memories were hard to bear. There's something behind the eyes that gives them away.

To an observer like me it's as if they have to, *need* to do this every once in a while. But they only ever go so far. There's an invisible line they never cross when they're recounting their time in action. I excused myself and left them to it. I ran a bath and took a book to bed. I could still hear their quiet voices below as my eyelids began to droop.

I had an early shift next morning so I didn't see Ian. I guessed he'd had a late night sitting up talking with Alex Scott as Ian had gone into the spare room to sleep so's not to wake me when he came up. I hoped the man-to-man talk had been good for both of them. I knew how much Ian had suffered after he came back from the Falklands. God knows how much Alex must have witnessed. I wondered was that why he'd wanted to be a blood donor.

I texted Kirsty later in the morning, just a quick message to tell her to remember to eat. She texted back,

Yes, Mum.

I wasn't about to take her word for it so that afternoon after work I drove round there to check on her. She buzzed me up and I let myself in. As I drew close I heard voices. Her door was ajar. I walked in.

Kirsty and Alex Scott were in her kitchen making hot drinks.

"Kirsty!" I said a little too loudly. "Are you all right?"

"Look who I found in the street," she said. "Coffee, Denise?"

I must have had a queer look on my face: Alex Scott began to explain.

He said, "I was in the newsagent on the corner when Kirsty came in."

"Milk," she interrupted. "I'd run out."

I knew straight away he must have been hanging around the area. It was obvious. What would he have done if Kirsty hadn't needed milk? I didn't say anything, though. They seemed to be getting along okay. I decided to bide my time and just see how things progressed.

We moved into Kirsty's sitting room and sat around her coffee table. They talked about small things: what they'd watched on television recently; a comparison of kitchen appliances as Alex was looking for a vacuum cleaner for his place; how Alex had come across the kitten up the tree. Kirsty told him about her friend Lizzie and the video she'd taken of the rescue. I sensed they were skirting around the issue they both needed to talk about.

"So, Alex," I said. "What made you decide to become a donor?"

That was when we all learned the truth about each other.

Alex Scott put down his cup and settled back into his seat.

"It's a long story," he said.

"I'm in no rush," I said. "Are you, Kirsty?"

She shook her head.

"I don't want to go into details," Alex began.

I said, "I understand."

He took a deep breath and looked as if he was going to speak. Then he bit his lip and his eyes clouded. He looked at his feet.

"I'm sorry I got so upset with you," Kirsty said then. "Only, when I learned you were a soldier it made me think about my brother. He wanted to be a soldier since he was just a little boy. He was over the moon when he was accepted."

Alex looked up from the floor and said, "What happened to him?"

"He died. He was only nineteen."

"Ah, Jesus," Alex said under his breath. He fixed his gaze on the blank television screen and let out a long sigh. "We were on patrol," he said. "We thought we'd cleared the area earlier but we were taking no chances. We had one of the young lads with us. Laugh a minute kind of guy. Classroom joker I bet he was when he was a kid. Real popular with all of us. I saw a flash in the distance. Sniper. I yelled at him to get down. Another flash and I threw myself on top of him. My arm was hurting like hell and then I must have passed out."

Kirsty and I waited for him to continue. I could tell he was searching for the right words, the best words to tell us what happened next but sparing us the worst.

I said, "Go on, Alex."

"I found out later he'd bled to death. I was out of it. Unconscious. We couldn't get him back to base in time to save his life," he said.

Kirsty said, "But you lost your arm trying to save him. You did what you could."

"It wasn't enough. What happened to your brother? Where was he?"

"He was still in training," Kirsty said. "He never got to be the real soldier he wanted to be. He had a heart problem none of us knew about. I wanted to know why it had never been picked up on any medical assessments but they said sometimes these things happen."

"I'm sorry for your loss," Alex said.

"Alex," I said, "I know you've probably heard this before but you mustn't blame yourself."

"It's hard not to. I should have been faster, sharper."

"You were all taking the same risks. But, listen to me. What do I know about it? I should keep my mouth shut. I know nothing about military life. Only what Ian's told me. But I know about people, Alex. I know when you harbour negative thoughts too long they can make you ill. You have your life to live. A chance for a fresh beginning."

The new beginning took many months for all three of us. My retirement day rolled around and we had the usual works' party at my choice of an Italian restaurant in town. Kirsty gradually regained her strength of spirit and went on to become team leader of her own unit. When British troops finally came out of Afghanistan Alex Scott started up his own property development business employing veterans to refurbish houses for injured service families. He often pops in to where I'm a volunteer worker at the British Legion charity shop. His eyes have lost that suspicious glare. He's more relaxed, more sociable. He comes with Ian and me on sponsored events, too, as does Kirsty when she's free. I watch them together sometimes. I think there might be a romance developing there. I hope so. You never know what's round the corner.

What's for Dinner?

The cure for boredom is curiosity. There is no cure for curiosity.

Dorothy Parker 1893- 1967 (attributed)

Janice wasn't concentrating on the conversation round the table in the coffee bar. Then Alison said something that struck home.

"Don't you just get tired of planning meals all the time?" she said. "Don't you just get absolutely sick to death of wondering what to do for dinner?"

The four women, all retired, met every other Saturday for shopping. At Alison's outburst Roz tittered in her usual non-committal way. In a discussion Roz changed sides like the wind. Diana smiled and said something comforting, the way she always did to diffuse strong feeling. But Alison's question had ignited a fire in Janice.

"Oh, yes," she said. "There are times when I'd be happy to fry an egg sandwich, or something, but if I did, I'd feel . . ."

"Guilty?" Alison said.

Janice felt her face grow hot. An upsurge of indignation twisted her insides. She didn't want to be comforted by Diana's soothing words. She didn't want to sit on the fence, avoiding difficult subjects like Roz. Janice wanted to let it all out.

"I'm sixty three," she said. "I've been planning meals for forty years, and to be honest, I've had enough."

Roz took a bite of her toasted sandwich. Diana sipped her hot chocolate. People streamed in and out of the coffee bar. The door opened and closed with a clunking sound. The cappuccino machine hissed. Roz munched. Diana sipped.

Alison said, "So, what are you going to do about it?"

They were all three staring at her. The coffee bar and its customers, its noises and smells faded into a blurred background like a scene in a movie. Three faces were in sharp focus waiting for her reply. Alison had started it but, somehow, it had become Janice's responsibility to find an answer.

She said, "I'm going to take some time out."

She fried egg sandwiches that evening for supper. Her husband looked down at his plate and back up again at Janice.

"Could I have some bacon with that?" he said.

"Yes, Stephen," she said. "You know where it is."

And she stayed at the table while Stephen went to the fridge for the bacon. By the time he'd grilled it his egg was cold and he complained.

Janice said, "What a shame."

On Sunday Stephen went for his hour's cycle ride and brought back the paper. He sat in the conservatory reading for another hour then had a half hour on the phone with his brother in Scotland. At twelve thirty he wandered into the kitchen.

"Enjoy your morning?" Janice said, peering over the top of a novel.

"What are you doing?" he said.

"I'm reading a book."

"Yes, I can see that."

"So, why did you ask? Did you really mean to say what am I *not* doing, Stephen?"

She saw him looking at the oven which was silent and cold.

"What's for dinner?" he said.

Janice put down her book and looked him square in the eyes.

"I don't know," she said.

"But I'm feeling a bit hungry."

"Help yourself, darling. I don't fancy a big roast dinner today." And she buried her nose in her book.

It took him till Thursday to ask her what was the matter.

It wasn't a comfortable settlement. Janice and Stephen had to address things they hadn't talked about for years: boredom and the frequency of it; money and the shortage of it; sex and the lack of it.

Janice said, "We've got out of the habit of talking to each other, Stephen. Since we retired, we bumble about."

"Bumble about?" he said. "I don't bumble."

"But you do. And so do I. You do your thing. I do mine. We don't do anything together any more. I don't want to spend the rest of our lives bumbling."

On Friday Janice filled in a form for senior citizens' reduced prices at the cinema and Stephen agreed to go see a film once a month. On Saturday she got out a cookery book and Stephen chose a new recipe to try. He went to buy the ingredients while Janice did the ironing. On Sunday Janice got out her bike and rode with him. By the time Monday rolled around they'd run out of things to talk about. Tuesday was an effort and Wednesday was a strain.

"This is not working, is it?" Janice said.

Stephen scratched his head and looked shame-faced.

"Not really," he said. "I think I was happier before."

"Hmmm," she said.

***

"So, how did it go?" Alison asked at the next Saturday meeting in the coffee bar. She leaned forward across the table, her fingers clasped tightly. Her voice was full of expectation. Diana and Roz were all eyes and ears, their toast and hot drinks left untouched.

"It wasn't about planning meals," Janice said. "That was just a symptom. Stephen and I are working on it. Thanks for asking."

She picked up her coffee.

Silence. Three disappointed faces.

"Is that it?" Alison asked, dissatisfaction written all over her face.

"Yes," Janice said. "Realistically, you can't expect to fix in a week what's taken years to build up in the first place." She smiled at them and took a sip.

Diana said, "Ah", the way you'd coo at a baby. Roz made a humming noise as if she understood exactly what Janice was saying but her face was a picture of uncertainty.

"So, you haven't found the answer?" Alison said.

Was that a flicker of resentment glittering in Alison's eyes? What had they expected Janice to say?

She put down her cup.

"We're talking," she said. "As I said, we're still working on it. Isn't that what we all have to do?"

Their disillusioned faces fell further. Janice picked up her cup again and would say no more. It made her smile to think about Stephen at home in his shed happily fixing a puncture on her bike. The others would have to find their own answers. As far as Janice was concerned there was comfort, after all, in bumbling.

Lemon Meringue

If suffer we must, let's suffer on the heights.
Victor Hugo 1802-1885

My sister is dithering. She pays no heed to the long line of people behind us with their empty trays, or to the clock, or the background music that has ended one movie theme and is well into another. Her eyes are vacant. She can't see the kid serving at the cake counter who is tapping her feet and looking agitated beneath her swept-back *Breakfast at Tiffany* hairstyle and matte red lipstick. My sister can't make up her mind. She's staring through and beyond all the pretty portions in frosted triangles, decorated cup cakes on their shiny china plates and creamy pots of puddings.

She's hesitant about everything these days. See, I'd know not to give her too many choices or else we'd hold up the queue till tomorrow while she decides whether it's to be a chocolate muffin or vanilla or something else entirely. But the assistant at the counter has offered too many things and Donna can't decide.

"You always enjoy lemon meringue, Donna," I suggest.

"Well, yes, I know I do, but I wonder if I might enjoy cheesecake more this afternoon." She looks at the assistant. "What kinds of cheesecake did you say you have?"

"Strawberry, raspberry or mandarin."

"No blackcurrant?"

"No."

"Are those pieces of mandarin on top of the cheesecake out of a tin?"

"I don't know."

"Because, you see, it does make a lot of difference, you know."

"Why don't you have lemon meringue today, Donna" I say.

"But I was going to have cheesecake."

"Yes, but the assistant doesn't know if the fruit is fresh or canned."

"Couldn't she go and ask somebody?"

The assistant pipes up. "I'm not allowed to leave the counter." She puts her hands on her hips and her head does that rocking from side to side thing. I didn't quite see so I can't be certain, but I think she rolled her eyes first.

"She's not allowed to leave the counter, Donna, and the strawberries *and* the raspberries might be out of a can, too."

"Oh, well," Donna says, "if it isn't fresh fruit . . ."

A man in the queue behind us is coughing and shuffling his feet.

"Come on, Grandma," he says. "We haven't got all day."

Donna turns to face him. Her eyes are smiling and her face is kind.

"Young man, nobody knows how long any of us have got," she says.

"Come on, Donna," I say. "The lemon meringue does look particularly good."

"You're right, Victoria." She leans toward the assistant. "I'll take a piece of lemon meringue, please."

We find an empty table near a window. There's a view of the cobbled courtyard out the back with pots of summer things that have blossomed and faded. Inside, the walls are decorated with black and white photos of movie stars from the 1940s, 50s and 60s when Hollywood stardom attracted heavenly devotion from film-goers. Film stars looked like film stars then. Apparently that era is trendy again judging by Audrey Hepburn on the cake counter and Lauren Bacall at the cash desk.

I sit. I have to wait for Donna to get comfortable. I look at the pictures on the walls so I don't have to witness the rigmarole she goes through. I'm listing the names of all these old movie stars and trying to remember titles of favourite films but out of the corner of my eye I can still see Donna fussing over the table before she sits down.

Doris Day - Calamity Jane - a special favourite of mine - Donna brings out a tissue,

James Dean - East of Eden - and wipes the table with it.

Jane Russell -oh, what's it called; the one where she wears that low cut blouse on the poster - *The Outlaw* - another tissue to finish polishing the table- and another tissue

Rock Hudson - to rub at our pastry forks and spoons before putting them back on the tray.

They are her little rituals now, these habits. They are things she does while her thinking is catching up with the situation she's in.

I suppose she must be telling herself *I'm in the café and I'm getting ready to eat something.*

The music segues into a new theme.

John Wayne is looking down at me from under his stetson.

Why are they playing Pirates of the Caribbean? I'm thinking, shouldn't it be something else? What would be more appropriate to match these faces on the wall? Can you download theme tunes from old Hollywood movies?

I can stop filling my head with distracting thoughts now; Donna has finished. She's putting her pack of tissues away and is closing her handbag. I smile at her. She puts her handbag on the floor and pulls out her chair. The handbag is in her way now so she picks it up again.

"Shall I hold that for you? Till you're in."

She hands me the bag, sits and pulls in the chair a little. She half gets up and smooths her skirt before sitting down again.

"These places never give you enough space," she grumbles, but she says it brightly, with shining eyes in her nodding head and a small smile so it doesn't sound or look like a complaint. My stomach sinks.There was a time when she would have made her feelings clear, no messing. She would have roared her aggravation and I would have withered beside her magnificence. Now, she seems apologetic and shrunken when she adds, "I bet people knock things over in here all the time."

I grab the plastic menu holder and move it to one side. Donna hasn't noticed how perilously close to her elbow it is. If it falls it will take out everything on our tray and both our pieces of lemon meringue could end up on the floor. Finally, she is settled. I put our handbags under the table at our feet and empty the tray.

The room is humming with muted conversations and movie music and near the cash desk a coffee machine is hissing white noise. Donna takes up her spoon and carefully removes her meringue topping. I watch her take her first mouthful of pastry and lemon filling . . .

. . . It has all come too soon. I don't want my big sister to grow old like this before my eyes, before her time. I haven't had long enough to be her sister. I'm not ready to give her up. I listen to the swish of the door as customers leave and more come in and I turn my head away because my eyes are brimming.

"Didn't we get any cream to go with this?" she asks me. "I always like to have a little dollop of cream with lemon meringue."

"It comes in these plastic pots," I say, grateful for something to do, holding one out to show her. I don't know whether to offer to open it for her. I'm not sure if we've reached that stage yet.

"Would you open that for me, Victoria?" she says. "I'm all thumbs just now and anyway, I'd need my other glasses out of my bag."

"No problem," I say with another smile, but it is a problem because it breaks my heart that my sister can't open a little pot of cream any more. I find the tab, pull back the foil lid and hand the pot to Donna.

"What is it?" she asks. "What's this?"

There's a huge lump forming at the back of my throat.

"It's cream, Donna. Put it on your lemon meringue."

She does. And tucks in.

I'm finding it hard to swallow mine. I look at the photos on the wall again and concentrate on waiting for the swish of the door.

She seems happy, though. Happy enough, I suppose. She smiles more now than ever she did before.

"That man in the queue behind us," she says. "I know him."

"Do you?"

"And his father."

"Do you?"

I never know whether I am meant to ignore things like this. Am I supposed to tell Donna she's mistaken or do I go along with whatever she says?

"Yes. I know them both."

"I don't think he's with anybody, Donna. I don't think his father is here."

"No. His father is dead. I used to teach them both."

It is a possibility.

"Did you?" I say.

"Little monkeys, the pair of them. He was just like his father. Always ready to make mischief."

It's ten years since Donna was diagnosed and retired early from teaching on the grounds of her ill health. The man in the queue would have been about sixteen then. It *is* a possibility that Donna knows him, but seems unlikely. People alter so much in that time. How could Donna recognise him? I wait to see if she changes the subject. She often flits from one conversation to another. It's a coward's way out for me when I don't know what to say next.

"Peter, his name was."

"Who? The young man in the queue?"

"No, his father." She spoons up another large piece of pie. It's too big, even without the meringue topping. She should have broken it in two, or should I have done that for her? I don't know. I can't tell from one day to the next what stage we're at with this thing. When *is* the right time for me to cut up my sister's pie? Am I supposed to wait until there's an embarrassing incident? Nobody tells you how you're supposed to react. And anyway, which one of us would be embarrassed? Donna wasn't the least bothered by her fussing over the cutlery and table with her packet of tissues. I reach for the teapot.

"Are you ready for a cup of tea now, Donna?" I say.

Her mouth is full. She chews slowly and deliberately as if she's only just learning how to do it. I realise my timing is poor. I should have remembered how slowly she eats. I should pay more attention. By the time she's finished chewing she will have forgotten what I said and I'll have to ask again. Why am I making such a big thing of it? Why don't I simply pour us both a cup of tea and she'll drink hers when she's ready. I'm annoyed with myself and, I'm ashamed to admit, I'm annoyed with Donna. She's eating her pie and looks as if she hasn't a care in the world. Whereas, me?

My throat is tight with the pain of it. How can Donna look so composed when, day by day, she is being stripped of herself? She used to be as sharp as the filling in that lemon meringue. Now look at her. Where is my sister? I want her back. I want to hear that edge in her voice, her dry wit. Even her cutting sarcasm. The way she could startle you with her abruptness, her matter of fact, no-nonsense attitude. I want back the sister who . . . And I know that's never going to happen.

"Excuse me," a voice says. I look up. It's the man from the queue. "Excuse me," he says again, looking straight at Donna, "but aren't you Miss Simpson?"

She smiles at him and nods.

"You used to be my English teacher," he says.

She smiles and gives him another benevolent nod.

"My sister has been unwell," I say. I always put it like that as if she's somehow on the mend and won't continue getting worse.

"I remember your classes, Miss Simpson. You're the only teacher who ever got me to read a whole book. I'm sorry I was a bit rude in the queue just now."

Donna puts down her spoon. She lifts her chin and looks him square in the eye.

"Not half as fucking rude as you fucking used to be," she says and slaps the table. "I've waited a lifetime to say something like that," she adds and cracks up laughing, still hammering the table.

He laughs with her and says, "Glad to see you're feeling better."

See, I don't know where I am with her from one day to the next. I can't be certain if what she's telling me is the truth or it's come out of a brain whose synapses are not firing properly. She's sitting there, chuckling to herself and I have to admit she does seem happier now than at any other time in her life.

For myself, I'm reminded of the way I felt the first time I went to see the musical *Les Miserables,* when in the middle of the tragedy of death after death there comes the song *Master of the House* and the audience gasps at the relief of having something to laugh at.

"Did you enjoy your pie?" she says.

"Yes. Didn't you? You haven't eaten the topping."

She grins. "Ah, but you know why, though, don't you?"

And I think I do.

My sister is just like the pie except the firm pastry base has gone out from under her. She's heading toward not being able to support herself. She's had the stuffing knocked out of her as well. She's losing substance, the very essence, juice and zest of her is being sucked away. She's like what's left on her plate: the whipped topping. Egg whites and sugar, light and fluffy, an insubstantial crisp of a thing, too sweet.

"Mmm," she says as she starts in on the meringue. "I'm saving the best for last."

Yorkshire Grit

Life does not cease to be funny when people die any more than it ceases to be serious when people laugh.

George Bernard Shaw 1856-1950

We're on Brow Top Road in The Three Sisters at a table by the big picture window overlooking moorland. It's early evening, almost dark. A March gale is turning the landscape inside out. Scrubby trees thrash in the winds. The Pennines are roaring winter's end. The room is too warm for my thick jacket but my heart is cool and quiet as the prints on the wall behind me of the famous sisters: Charlotte, with her ruffled collar and school mistress expression; Emily with a faraway look in her eyes and Anne of the Titian curls.

"We're just like the Brontës," my sister says.

"How do you mean?"

"Plotting."

I laugh. She laughs. My daughter looks at us both and grins. Here we are, the three of us, plotting certainly, but not for fiction. This is heart-stopping reality. It's why we have to keep cool heads as well as strong hearts. We've all practised stealth we never knew we possessed. And patience.

"Drink up, ladies," I say. "It's my round."

"Not here, Mum," Carla says. "Let's move on. To Haworth, right? We'll do the main street and have a drink in them all."

"Are you up for that?" Lucy says to her. "You'll be okay to drive back?"

"No problem. I want to keep a clear head for tomorrow when we . . . you know."

We don't talk about our plans any more. All the talking's done. We've hammered out every detail. Tomorrow we're going to break the law and that's all there is to it.

Out across the car park and the weather's raging fit to knock me off my feet.

"I'd forgotten how wild it can be up here," I say when we're buckled in with the car doors closed and they can hear me above the howling wind.

"Ah, you've gone soft, you two, living down south," Carla says.

We begin in The Fleece. There are some faces Carla knows. She stays at the bar chatting. I look around. I don't recognise anybody. My generation is at home with their slippers and cocoa.

I can feel Lucy staring at me. Sixteen years younger than me she looks more than ever like our mother in her warm winter coat and woolly scarf. My surprise sister. *Caught on the change* is how my mother explained it. Lucy grew up with parents old enough to be her grandparents, destined to lose both of them when her adulthood had only just begun. Her eyes are as soft as mum's were, questioning, pushing into my thoughts like mushrooms through cracks in concrete.

"What?" I say.

"You're different."

"I know."

"We're doing the right thing."

"I know we are."

"It's what he wanted."

I nod.

"Carla won't say anything to them up at the bar, will she?" Lucy asks.

"No. She won't do that. She's told nobody. She wouldn't spoil it now." I take hold of my little sister's hand and stroke it. "You were right all along, Lucy," I say. "All those years. I'm sorry I didn't listen to you."

"You were thinking about Dad. You did what you thought was best."

My sister's magnanimity continues through the evening. As does Carla's ebullience, in and out of The Black Bull, The King's Arms and The Old White Lion, my old stomping grounds in the days when I imagined myself invincible, when

I could run up Haworth main street at least part of the way without having to stop for breath and not worry about slipping on wet cobbles on the way down.

By the time we make it back to the car there's nothing else Lucy or I can remember about our separate Yorkshire childhoods. We've compared and contrasted everything. Carla's eyes look heavy; she's had a full day at work. When we tumble into her kitchen she makes her excuses and goes to bed.

Lucy fetches the bottle of brandy we brought with us.

"Come on," she says. "What shall we drink to?"

"Success tomorrow?"

"Sweet, sweet revenge," she says. "The only sweet stuff that isn't fattening."

"Who said that?"

"Alfred Hitchcock."

"Perfect."

*

We've made a large hole in the brandy, but I don't feel tired. I'm set on tomorrow. I can see everything in my mind's eye. I just want it to be over. Finished. Then we can get on with our lives again.

"It's going to feel bloody good," Lucy says, hugging the sofa cushions to her chest. "Bitch. How could she treat us like that?"

"Because she doesn't care. You were right, Lucy. She's always hated us and everything we stand for."

"Why?"

"Because Dad loved us. We're creative and clever like him. Hannah was jealous."

"You mean we've got a full set of brain cells and she hasn't?"

I smile. We've grown very free with our condemnation of the woman who married our father less than two years after Mum died. Dad was nearly seventy, his new wife a widow, twenty years younger. She isn't much older than I am. Lucy detested her and made no secret of it, whereas, me?

"She's a witch," Lucy used to say. "Haven't you seen how she's removed all his pictures of you and me and his grandkids? Replaced them all with her lot."

"It can't be easy for her," I'd say, trying to keep the peace, hoping things would work out in the end. But drop by venomous drop she did her utmost to poison our father against us. He used to send my children their birthday presents in secret so *she* didn't know.

I swallowed my feelings and let things be. I thought that was the right thing to do; not cause problems for him. When Lucy spoke her mind Hannah would go running off to him and make out she'd been verbally abused. Not in those words. She wouldn't have used those words. She probably doesn't even know what they mean. No. She'd go slinking off with tears in her snake eyes and make out Lucy had been horrible to her.

Dad took Hannah's side. I couldn't blame him. She was the one who was feeding him, washing his clothes, cleaning his house. I understood he didn't want her upset. He didn't want the hassle so he went for the easy option.

"She looks after him, Lucy," I'd say. "Neither of us can, can we? You're in Wiltshire. I'm in Norfolk. We wouldn't want him to be on his own, would we?"

"No, but, she's taking over everything," she'd say.

I know now my sister was right. The hag played us. Not as dumb as she looks. She played a very clever game driving wedges between us, telling tales, stirring her witches' brew, keeping her poisons bubbling.

I remember driving up from Norfolk for a visit just before Christmas one year to take up Dad's and her gifts. She showed me the fabulous things she was wrapping for her family. I admired them.

"Oh," she said. "I'm glad you like them. I wish your sister was more like you. I can't get on with her at all. She doesn't like me, you know. I don't know what I've done to offend her."

And I smiled at her and said something inane, the way I always did then. Fatuous but sincere as I could make it sound, saying anything to save my father's face. I should have said,

I'll tell you why Lucy's angry, Shitface. You've removed every trace of us from this house. His only grandson in his cap and gown on graduation day. What have you done with that photograph? Don't you know how proud my father was on that day?

Well, of course she knew how proud he was. She knew exactly what she was doing when she put that picture of Michael in the bin. She knew exactly what she was doing when she marched Dad off to the solicitor and got him to change his will. She *knew* she'd get the lot when he died.

None of us have anything that belonged to him. His World War Two service medals, promised to Michael? Disappeared. Rumour has it the witch gave them to *her* grandson. The antiquated pocket watch Dad used because wrist watches always went funny on him? Disappeared along with everything else. We haven't even got a handkerchief that was his.

When I think of the eulogy I read at the funeral service, especially the greasy inclusion of *Family Hag* and how they'd made my father happy in his later years, there's a hard lump comes into my throat that I'd like to spit into her face. I'd like to take her eye out with the velocity of a loaded gob of phlegm.

The worst thing she did to us was give us nowhere to go to remember him. We didn't know what she'd done with his cremated remains. In the end a neighbour told us. The witch was keeping them in the bottom of a wardrobe in her spare room out of our way. She wouldn't even let us have access to his final resting place. I don't have much respect for the law that can allow this kind of thing to happen. So, I don't care too much about breaking it tomorrow.

I know you're not supposed to seek revenge. They say it brings you down to the level of your adversary. Revenge can backfire and might result in things you never intended. But, there comes a time when you stop caring about these warnings. A line has been crossed. And yes, that's in the passive voice because you've stood back and let it happen. You've behaved passively, going with the flow, not rocking the boat and all those other clichés because, like an idiot, you've become a cliché yourself, thinking you're doing the right thing when all the time you've been getting it *so* wrong.

When I discovered Hannah had been telling everybody who would listen to her how little we had cared about our father, how we hardly ever went to see him, how we were mean to her and despised her family, more than ten years' worth of drowned disappointments rose to lodge in my throat like acid reflux. A volcano of hurt feelings vented and clung to my skin. My eyes burned under a glaze of sulphurous slime. For the first time in my life I wanted to get my own back.

It's good we kept connections with our Yorkshire roots. The fact that my daughter had returned there to work was a bonus. When the witch was planning to marry again we heard about it through those same connections she knew nothing about.

My need for revenge deepened. I imagined turning up at the wedding and spewing her poison back at her. On the phone Lucy and I joked about what we'd tell the hapless man's family, the things they could expect. We'd tell his children to take away their photographs and gifts to their father immediately before the witch got her hands on them. We'd warn them about the trip to the solicitor. We'd advise him to keep his money in his own name, separate from any joint accounts so she couldn't get at it.

And then it dawned on us. Where *were* our dad's ashes? Still at the bottom of a wardrobe? Was she going to hang on to them now she was getting married again? Making a scene at the wedding wasn't going to get us what we wanted. We held off. We waited. We didn't know where she'd moved or her new surname. My sister played detective and got in touch with all her old friends. It took over a year to get the information. A friend of a long line of friends had overheard a conversation in their local pub.

"Can you imagine what that must have been like?" Lucy says pouring another brandy for us both and getting comfortably mellow. "I mean, in the bar in front of everybody. I'd like to have been a fly on the wall. It's better than an episode of *Shameless*."

Only, it isn't funny. It's sick. Lucy's in a better place than I am. She's dealt with her anger and come out the other side of it. She can see beyond the indignity of what happened. I'm still plotting further revenge.

"The whole pub must have been ear-wigging," Lucy is saying. "*You'd better get shut of them ashes*," she says in a deep male voice with a pronounced Yorkshire accent. "*If you don't, I'm throwing 'em in the bin.*"

My father's ashes were handed over in the pub. Taken to the lounge bar, the casket in a supermarket carrier bag and handed over to Arbee like cheap meat from a horse butcher. Arbee had known our dad for years. He'd been the rag and bone man. R & B. Arbee. Nobody knows what his real name was. He used to go round the town with his horse and cart making a living out of other people's cast offs. A Romany, he could neither read nor write but he knew the proper thing to do and offered to take Dad's ashes off the hag's hands to prevent them going in the trash. That's how much *she'd* cared about him.

Lucy found Arbee's telephone number from somebody who knew his surname and called him. She said he sounded frail, his voice thin and tremulous.

"I knew somebody would come looking for him one day," he told her. "Well, I hoped so. Your father was a good man. There were not many in this town would pass the time of day with me, but your dad did. He always had time for me. I'd have got in touch with you or your sister but I didn't know how."

"Never mind," Lucy told him. "We can put it all to rights now."

The poor man was overjoyed Lucy had found him.

"I never liked her. That woman. Do you know what she's called on the estate? The Merry Widow. Everybody knows what she's like. A nasty piece of works."

"And she just wanted to get rid of my dad's ashes? Talking about it in the pub? Just like that?"

"She did. *I don't care what you do with them,* she said. *I don't want to know.* I suggested she get in touch with you. What about his daughters? I said to her, but she goes, *Oh, no. They're not having them.*"

"She said that?"

"Yes. So then I asked about taking him to your mother's grave. But she said she wasn't having that either."

"What did you do with him?" Lucy asked.

"He's in my allotment. Where I keep the horse."

"You scattered him?"

"No, no. I buried the casket. I'll dig him up for you, if you like. I always hoped you or your sister would come."

"My niece will come," Lucy told him. "She lives nearby. I'll give her your number so you can talk to her direct and make arrangements."

That was four months ago. We didn't know digging up interred *cremains* was illegal. We didn't stop to think about it. Burying them in council owned land without permission was a crime in the first place but we didn't know that either.

Carla collected her grandfather and has been *homing* him, she says, until we could all take time off from work and be together. Poor Arbee. Three weeks later he was dead. Digging up my father's remains must have been one of the last things he ever did.

So now my sister and I are sitting on my daughter's sofa, sipping good brandy. In the corner of the room is a plastic bag. Tomorrow we'll take it with us to the cemetery. We know now the law would not approve of what we're going to do with it.

❋

Breakfast is cooking. I feel hungry but there's a sour knot in my stomach. I stare out the window. Last night's gale has blown itself out. The air is still, the sky a sweaty grey like soiled bed linen. Carla is busy making bacon sandwiches. Lucy is gathering our things and checking everything's where it should be.

"You alright, Mum?" Carla says. "You're very quiet this morning. Did you have too much to drink last night?"

"It's not enough."

"What's not enough?"

"This. What we're doing."

Lucy says,

"Sit down and have a hot drink. What's on your mind?"

"*Are* we doing the right thing?"

"Of course we are. It's what Dad wanted. He told Arbee years ago."

"Might not be what Mum wanted, though."

Lucy looks at me as if I've said something terrible. Her eyes are wide and frightened and her mouth has fallen open. In that moment I know I must make a choice.

"Oh, take no notice of me," I say, falling back into my old pattern. "I'm just getting the jitters, that's all."

And the moment passes. I'm keeping the peace again because Lucy and I have such different memories. I don't want to spoil hers. Soon, we're wrapped in coats and scarves and on our way.

The road climbs to a steep bank of moorland. The lodge is right by the cemetery gates and we have to ring for admittance by car.

"Bit better than yesterday," the lodge keeper says as he lets us in. "But you'll have to leave the car down this end this morning, my love. There's a big branch to clear from the path higher up. Came down last night in the wind."

I didn't plan on this. I thought we'd be able to drive half way up the hill away from the lodge as usual. I keep my face straight as I get out and walk to the rear of the car. Lucy and Carla follow my lead. We grab our stuff from the boot. The lodge keeper is watching us.

"You've got your hands full there, ladies," he says, eyeing the plastic buckets and scrubbing brushes. My stomach lurches.

It's a criminal offence to dig into a grave even if the plot contains your mother and all you're going to do is put your father's ashes in there. You have to apply for permission. Some stranger has to come to see the job's done properly.

"Yes. We've come to give Mum's headstone a good spring clean," I say, the practised words sounding full of enthusiasm, bright and crisp. "White marble. You know how it looks after a long winter."

The trowels are at the bottom of the buckets hidden with the casket underneath cleaning fluid and rags. I make a show of checking the contents of my bucket as if I'm looking for something. My hand finds a trowel handle and I grasp it. I'm concentrating on not letting my face slip. We have a job to do. The earth is soft now; it's why we waited till winter had passed. We should be able to do this. I move off.

"Whatever you do, don't look back," I say. "Act normal."

It's a steep climb. We walk slowly, the buckets' contents clattering. There's a figure standing waiting by the halfway bench.

Carla suddenly stops.

"It's Michael," she cries out and runs up the hill to greet her brother. "You made it!"

My sister turns to me.

"Did you know he was definitely coming?" she says. "He's flown in specially?"

"Yes. Surprise. He has to go straight back, though."

With kisses and hugs we gather by the bench at the bottom of the final rise to Mum's grave. It occurs to me we don't know who the plot belongs to now. Legally, I suppose it's Hannah the Hag's because she inherited everything that was Dad's, even what's left of my mother.

"I'm so glad you could get away, Michael," I say when all the catching up questions are done.

"Wouldn't miss this," he says and gives everybody another quick hug. "But I can't stay long." The others don't notice the way he winks at me. "I wonder what she'd say if she could see us now?"

"Who? Grandma?" Carla says.

"No. Hannah. She wouldn't know which one of us to have a go at first. Here, Mum, give me that bucket. I'll carry it."

"Ah, she wouldn't pick on you, Michael," Lucy says. "You were always Dad's favourite."

"You're wrong, there. She always pretended to make a fuss of me whenever I went to visit but as soon as I'd gone she moaned about me to Mrs Spencer next door."

"No." Lucy bites at her lip.

"Oh, yes. She complained about me eating them out of house and home, apparently, but all I can remember being given is a few slices of toast."

"And Dad knew she was criticising even you?"

"I think so. She did it to all of us, didn't she? Nice as pie to your face then daggers in your back. She'd say to me what a lovely lad I was. And why couldn't my mother and the other one be more like me."

"The *other one*? Is that what she called me?"

"She did a proper number on us, Lucy. I'm glad we're getting one over on her now."

Lucy sinks onto the bench. Michael sits beside her.

"I just can't believe he knew about it all the time and said nothing to her," she says, her voice directed to the sky. Her eyes are moist. "Why didn't he sort her out? Why didn't he stick up for *us*?"

I sit and put my arm around her shoulder.

"I can believe it," I say. "I'm sorry, Lucy, but that's the choice he made. It was easier for him to hurt us to keep her sweet. He knew we'd always stand by him."

"Nobody ever made Granddad do anything he didn't want to do," Carla says. "Grandma told me that."

Carla's words are like the moment the sun breaks through after fog. It happens slowly. You can tell there's a difference but the developing brightness is incremental, so gradual it's hard to pinpoint the exact moment when the fog's completely gone and what you've got is crystal clear reality after years of pretending.

We clean Mum's headstone, scrubbing and rubbing till our hands are red with cold. We stand back to look at it. Glinting in thin sunlight, white Italian marble from her favourite holiday destination marks her journey into eternity.

"Grandma would have hated Hannah," Carla says. "They'd never have been friends."

I agree. "He got what he wanted in the end," I say. "What are we going to do with him now?"

"If we don't bury the ashes," Lucy says, "Hannah wins again."

"She won't know though, will she? Either way. Whatever we do, she's never going to know." Carla says. "And anyway, this is not about Hannah, is it? We do what *we* think is the right thing."

At the back of the cemetery there's a small gate leading out onto a rough track into the moors. The ground is springy beneath our feet. We take out the pouch of ashes from its casket. Amongst crunchy bracken and heather still brown and bare we set him free, the Yorkshire grit of him falling into the heath.

Michael has to leave. He takes with him the earth-dampened and damaged empty casket wrapped in a plastic carrier bag.

"What do you want that for?" Lucy says. "It doesn't mean anything now."

"There's something I have to do before my return flight," Michael says. "Mum will tell you all about it later. Look, I'll stay longer next time. I promise."

We wave him off in his hire car. The three of us have a table booked for a celebratory lunch. I fend off questions about Michael's mysterious announcement.

"It's a pity he couldn't join us for a meal before he left," Carla says.

"Yes," I say. "I hardly ever get to see you both in the same place at the same time."

We're part way through dessert at two pm. when my cell phone text beeps as arranged.

It's done, he writes. *Tell Lucy and Carla. Enjoy your champagne dinner. See you again soon. Love you.*

I read out the message.

"What's done?" Lucy asks.

"Our sweet revenge." I take my time to savour the moment. It's better than *crème brûlée*. I lick my lips to taste the words. "Hannah is going to get a message. From beyond the grave."

"What message? Who's going to give it to her?" Lucy asks.

"Dad is." I can feel my wicked grin stretching my face.

"What?"

It's an effort not to crack up. I want to laugh, crow, howl the news, but I rein myself in and keep my voice low.

"Michael's been to visit an old friend this afternoon," I tell them. "Billy Hardacre's grandson. He used to play Dungeons and Dragons with Michael when they were kids. They've been in touch with one another for some time now. Would you believe it, he can't stand the woman his grandfather married last year. Hannah."

I lean back in my seat and enjoy watching their eyes open wider as they realise where this is going.

"Yes," I go on. "Apparently, the dreadful woman is causing all kinds of problems in their family. Michael's friend is worried on behalf of his mother. Hannah is stirring up trouble and telling lies. Well, we all know where that leads, don't we? So between them Michael and his friend thought of a way to pay her back."

"What's he done? Come on, Mum, I'm dying to know."

Carla can hardly sit still.

"Michael said he was very willing. Had a plan all worked out. Couldn't wait to do it."

"Do what?"

"Michael gave him your granddad's casket. They put some fresh cinders in it."

"Cinders? What for?"

"To cause problems. To give *her* some explaining to do. He's going to wait for the right time, though, before he makes his move."

I can tell by the Mona Lisa smile on Lucy's face she's already worked it out.

Carla says, "What is he going to do?"

"He's going to sneak Granddad's casket back in the bottom of Hannah's wardrobe."

January Girl

The worst loneliness is not to be comfortable with yourself.
Mark Twain 1835-1910

Lisa bent down to pick up a pink envelope from the doormat. *For the birthday girl* was printed on the front. The back showed the logo of the online card company. She sighed.

Here we go again, she thought. She put it on the hall stand and hurried out to catch the bus for the first day back at work after the holiday. There was just enough time to buy some mints and a newspaper from the corner shop. She grabbed a magazine as well.

"I gave you a twenty," she said, holding out her hand for the rest of her change. The girl opened the cash drawer. Lisa leaned over the counter to see inside. "There you are, look," Lisa said. "There's a twenty on top of the tens."

The girl shrugged and said, "Sorry." It didn't sound sincere.

January girls were born to be short-changed, Lisa thought. It was their role in life and every year when the birthday rolled around again the lack of enthusiasm from friends and family provided the first of the New Year's disappointments.

Lisa watched the houses flash past the bus window. It had begun to rain. Soon the glass would steam up and there'd be nothing to look at.

In two days' time, I'll be fifty, she thought. *Thirty years of sitting on this bus and looking at those same houses.*

The windows steamed up.

A woman got on at the next stop and sat beside her. She looked about Lisa's age. Lisa recognised the green raincoat the woman was wearing. There was a tiny scorch mark on the left cuff where Lisa had caught it on the gas hob. That wasn't the reason she'd taken it to the charity shop, though. It was too big and the sleeves were too long. Losing weight had happened so rapidly after Jonathan left.

"You don't want to lose any more weight," her sister, Jeanette, had told her. "It's not an attractive look when you're getting older. It makes your nose look big."

The pink envelope would be from Jeanette. There'd be a funny card inside, one of those with a picture on the front that looks like it's been taken from a 1950's knitting pattern. There wouldn't be a fancy gift. January girls miss out on special birthday presents.

When Lisa was a child her Christmas presents would arrive with *'and this is for your birthday, too.'* It still happened. She'd once said to Jonathan, "How would you like it if I gave you a Christmas present and said *and this is for your birthday, too?"*

"That's different," he said. "My birthday's in July."

"Well, mine's on January fourth. You know, when nobody has any energy left to celebrate."

"They haven't got any money left either," he'd replied.

The woman in the seat next to Lisa started fiddling with her cuff. Out of the corner of her eye, Lisa could see her folding under the sleeve to hide the scorch mark. Lisa turned away and pretended to look out but the glass was misted like a shower screen. As the bus picked up speed rain lashed at the windows and ran in horizontal squiggles.

Birthdays ending in a zero were worst of all. When Lisa was ten, all she'd wanted was a tennis racquet.

"But it's the middle of winter," her mother had said. "You can't play tennis now."

When she was twenty her husband of two weeks had thought it a good idea to spike her drink and she'd thrown up all over her new suede coat. When she was thirty her divorce from said husband became absolute. On the day of her fortieth birthday, on the *actual* day, a nice surgeon had taken away her insides to prevent proliferation of rogue cells. Jeanette had come to visit and brought cream cakes. Lisa was still groggy from the anaesthetic and in too much pain to eat cake. Nobody thought to save any for her for later.

Now she was two days away from the big five-oh, on her own again, too skinny and with a big nose.

"Excuse me," the woman in the next seat said. "Don't you work at Marks and Spencer?"

"Yes, that's right."

The woman ran a hand over the front of her coat. Her nails were bitten and ugly. Her fingers stained by nicotine.

"This is from Marks and Spencer, you know."

"Is it? It's very nice. Ideal for this weather. The colour suits you very well."

"It isn't new."

"No? I'd never have guessed."

"Got it from the charity shop. You know, the one that supports the hospices." "

"I know the one you mean."

"I always like to support the hospices."

"Yes. So do I."

The woman reached into the handbag on her knee and brought out her purse. She removed a photograph.

"This is my Richard. He's gone now. I don't know what I would have done without the hospice."

Lisa's skin prickled. She brought her hand to her mouth. She knew her ex-husband had married again but she thought he'd moved to another district. She hadn't seen him in years. But there he was in this woman's photograph of him, still with the same flop of hair, holding his head to one side in that self-conscious way he had whenever someone pointed a camera at him.

"I lost my husband too," Lisa said.

"I know. You're Lisa, aren't you? Richard's first wife."

Lisa's stomach somersaulted. This was the weirdest conversation. Yet, somehow, it felt comforting. There was no malice in the woman's face, no spite in the tone of her voice. Her eyes were warm and kind. Before Lisa realised what she was doing she was opening her heart to a kind stranger on the bus.

"Sometimes," Lisa said, "sometimes, I pretend Jon left me. You know, that he's still alive somewhere, being happy."

"They say time is the best healer. I'm still waiting for it to happen to me."

"How did you know?" Lisa said.

"About you and your husband? Richard used to point you out whenever we came to Marks and Spencer."

"You live locally? I don't remember ever seeing him in the shop."

"Oh, he wouldn't come in. He used to wait outside. He didn't like shopping. Did your husband like shopping?"

"Jonathan hated it."

The bus turned the corner and slowed for the bus station in the centre of town. Passengers got up and formed a queue down the central aisle.

"Well, it's been nice talking to you, Lisa," the woman said as she joined the others waiting to alight.

Lisa said, "Perhaps I'll see you again next time you're out shopping." She reached down and collected her bag from the floor by her feet as the woman shuffled along in the aisle waiting her turn to get off.

"I don't think so. I'm leaving soon. I sold the house. I couldn't stay there on my own. I'm going back to Devon. You know, to be closer to my family. Anyway, I hope you have a Happy Birthday."

Lisa sat bolt upright. Cold chills ran along her back and up into her hairline. She wanted to shout after the woman but realised she hadn't asked her name. Then, it was too late. The bus emptied and Lisa was the last to get off. The woman had disappeared.

The shop was busy all day with people bringing back things to exchange or wanting refunds for unwanted Christmas gifts. Lisa was glad of it: it left little time to think about the odd conversation on the bus and how the strange woman seemed to know so much about her.

After work she telephoned her sister. She thanked Jeanette for the card and related her mysterious morning journey.

"Does she always get on at that stop?" Jeanette said.

"No. I've never seen her before. I would have noticed the raincoat."

"It sounds to me like she planned it."

"Why would she do that?"

"What did she look like, Lisa?"

"About my age, my height, dark hair. A bit like me, really."

"I'll come round, Lisa. Put the kettle on."

***

Jeanette arrived with a bunch of freesias.

"I was going to wait till your birthday, Lisa," she said. "But I saw these on the way over and . . ."

"Thank you. Let me put them in some water."

Jeanette followed Lisa into her kitchen.

"So, this woman on the bus. She looked quite a lot like you?"

"Yes, I suppose you could say that. Especially in my old coat. Why? What do you know about her?" Lisa made tea. Jeanette made herself comfortable on a chair but looked as if she didn't know where to begin. "Come on, Jeanette. Out with it."

"It's only a theory, Lisa," Jeanette said.

"Let's hear it, then."

Jeanette took a deep breath and said, "I don't think Richard ever stopped loving you."

"What? Don't be silly, Jan. He got married again."

"To a carbon copy of you."

"I wouldn't go so far as to say that."

Jeanette shuffled in her seat and looked uncomfortable.

"I never told you before, but I used to see Richard in town . . ."

"There's nothing unusual about that but I thought he'd moved away. I never saw him."

"Let me finish, Lisa. I'd see him standing around outside Marks and Spencer. Every now and then he'd peer through the windows."

"He'd be waiting for his wife. She told me he didn't like going in shops with her."

"He was hoping to catch sight of *you.*" Jeanette held up her hand to stop her sister from interrupting again. "I saw him there a few times. Once, I waited out of sight."

"What for?"

"To see *her*. To see what she looked like. And then, each time I saw her after that, she looked more and more like you."

"I don't know what you mean."

"The first time I saw her she was fair-haired. Then she dyed it darker and had it cut in the same style as you."

"Is that it?"

"I know it doesn't sound like much. Lots of women have similar haircuts, but, honestly, it just didn't feel right. So I followed her."

"Jeanette!"

"I know, I know. But listen to this, Lisa. When she came into the shop, she was watching you. She'd stand behind you and watch how you walked and everything. I *saw* her. I think she was copying you, for him, to please him."

"That's terrible. The poor woman."

"And then she bought your coat."

"No. Now wait a minute. She couldn't possibly have known that was my coat in the charity shop."

"How do you know?"

Lisa searched her memory for the slightest thing, *anything* that might point to a time where they could have met before. How could she not have noticed? If the woman had been following her like Jeanette said, how could she not have felt *something*?

"Why didn't you tell me any of this before, Jeanette?"

"I would have if I'd thought there was real reason to bother you with it. How did she seem to you when you spoke on the bus?"

"She seemed very friendly. Sad, but not threatening in any way."

"That's what I thought, too. I think she must have had a lonely kind of marriage with him. Imagine what it must be like loving a man who wishes you were someone else."

"And then she lost him," Lisa said. "She doesn't even have the kind of memories I have."

The thought was unbearable.

The back door opened and suddenly the house was full of noise. Harry was back from swimming. His girlfriend, Donna was with him.

"Mum," he said. "We're starving. Hi, Jeanette."

They dumped their bags and rushed off to the sitting room.

"Bacon sandwiches?" Lisa shouted after them.

"Yes, please, Mrs Wilson," Donna shouted back.

"He's doing okay, isn't he?" Jeanette said.

"Yes. He's able to talk about his dad now. I think we're both on the mend."

Lisa got up and the smell of freesias wafted through the kitchen, like a breath of fresh air. In her imagination she could still see the woman in her second-hand coat, a terribly lonely woman planning to move away from the scene of her loveless life.

Lisa's eyes filled. She had known love. She'd had that precious gift. She still had it. Her son and his girlfriend, Donna were chatting in the sitting room. Jeanette had brought her pretty flowers and was here, smiling at her with sisterly love in her eyes.

Like Mother, Like Daughter

Advice is what we ask for when we already know the answer but wish we didn't.
Erica Jong 1942 -

My daughter was asking me for advice.

"Oh, Emily," I said. "I'm *so* not the right person to ask. I'm the last person to ask about *men*. You know that."

She shrugged and said, "I've already asked everyone else. So, you see, you *are* the last person I've asked."

I had to laugh. She looked at me through glinting steel eyes. In the tilt of her head and the tight shape of her mouth I saw myself thirty years before. I knew she'd keep on until I gave her an answer.

"Emily," I said. "Why *are* you asking me now? What have other people told you?"

We were at lunch in one of those places the office crowd frequent on weekdays, tucked into a cosy courtyard through an archway in the old part of the city. We'd been Saturday shopping together, something I *am* good at.

Emily put down her knife and fork and leaned toward me.

"Other people have all advised me to speak to you," she said.

"*All* of them?" I said, feeling a warm flush of pride that Emily's friends thought I was such an important part of her life. After all, I thought, mothers my age know they have to take a back seat in their daughters' lives. When daughters have babies of their own, that's when they come back to you for advice and support.

"Are you pregnant?" I said.

"No, mother. I'm not pregnant. I have an important decision to make and I'd like to hear what you think."

"About a man?"

"Yes."

"And the question is?"

"Should I move in with him?"

She took another mouthful of her food and munched on it, those eyes of hers wide and bright and difficult to read.

"It's very simple," I said. "If you have to ask that question, it's not the right thing for you to do."

"And you can say that even though you know nothing about the circumstances?"

"Absolutely. No doubt about it."

I thought the subject was finished. There was nothing to add. Emily had asked her question and I'd answered it. I finished my glass of Chardonnay.

"And you don't want to know anything about him?" Emily said. Her tone was accusing, her eyes steelier than ever.

"I've been abrupt, haven't I?" I said. "Sorry. Tell me about him."

"Well, he's a lot older than me."

"He isn't married, is he? Oh, Emily. Have you learned nothing from my mistakes?"

"No, Mum. He isn't married."

"Well, that's something, I suppose. But *much* older? Really?"

"It isn't about having a physical relationship."

"Good. It better hadn't be. They can't, you know. So what *is* it about?"

She took a moment to answer me, as if she was searching carefully for her words. She picked up the bottle we were sharing and poured me another half glass.

"I want to spend time with him," she said, avoiding my eyes, keeping her gaze firmly on the wine. "Get to know him."

"Spend *time* with him? *Spend time* with him? Emily, you're talking like an old woman. At your age you should be having fun, going places, learning new skills, tasting new things, seeing what . . ."

"Like you did at my age?"

"Yes. Well, no, not quite like that. No, I didn't mean that. Oh, dear. See, I told you I was the last person you should ask about relationships with men. I never got one of them right, did I?"

"You made me out of one of them."

"I did and you are the very best thing from all my failed relationships. You're the most important person in my life. I'm useless about men, Emily. You know that."

"Not one of them ever left you, Mum. You were always the one who walked."

She was right. I was a serial walker. Four temporarily serious relationships in a row. One daughter from the third one. Several silly dalliances in between. Was that so bad? I didn't keep in touch with any of them after I'd left. What was the point? They probably all had new partners. Why would they want to hear from me?

" . . . and there'll be economic benefits as well," Emily was saying. "I can't afford the apartment on my own, so . . ."

"Emily, you know you can come back to me."

"Not this time, Mum. We all have to move on, don't we?"

The waiter came to clear and we ordered coffee.

"He's coming here to meet you," Emily said.

"What? Now?"

"Yes. He said he wanted to see you again."

"Again? What do you mean *again*? I know him?"

"No you don't *know* him. You were never able to tell me much about him. You kept him out of my life. He didn't know about me. I found him online."

I had just realised who was coming to join us when there he was, standing beside Emily and with his hand on her shoulder.

"You're looking well, Barbara," he said to me.

"Malcolm," I said. "Hello."

He took a seat beside our daughter and I saw how their noses were exactly the same shape. She had his metal-coloured eyes, too. Both pairs were happy and smiling. I couldn't remember the last time Emily had looked at me like that.

"I thought you'd moved abroad, Malcolm," I said. "Selling time shares or something."

He laughed. "That's a long time ago. I have my own estate agency in Morocco. Very popular with the Irish just now."

"I've always wanted to see Marrakech," Emily said, gazing at her father.

Fear fluttered in my stomach.

She left with him. I watched them cross the road, arms linked, heads together.

She looks like him, but walks like me, I thought.

She walked beside her father, her long, easy strides matching his. She didn't look back.

The Fire Dragon

Employment is the surest antidote to sorrow.
Ann Radcliffe 1764-1823

Mark's good at fixing things around the house. That is to say, he's good at fixing things in other people's houses. Got a problem with your log burner? Mark's your man. Car won't start? He'll be there in five minutes. Plumbing, wiring, building, plastering, tiling? Send for Mark. He can do it all.

Three months ago, his son, Liam broke an ornament. It's a favourite of mine. My sister bought it for me: a small ceramic dragon, which burns incense cones in its pot belly so that perfumed smoke curls out of holes in its nostrils. It's got a friendly face and grey-green scales down its back and along its tail and wings.

"It's a fire dragon," Lucy said when she gave it to me. "He needs a name and a nice hearth to sit by. He'll look after you and wherever you go, you'll always have warmth."

My sister's always been a bit idealistic. She's given to romantic gestures and I love her for it. So do her husband and children. Duncan the dragon sat by my gas fire puffing out cinnamon scented smoke till I ran out of cones and by that time I'd met Mark and his son. I have no children of my own. When I was married I wasn't ready to start a family. I had my work; I illustrate gardening books, magazines and calendars. People think there has to be something wrong with a woman who doesn't want children. They say the rudest things behind your back. By the time I'd started thinking about babies, it was too late. The marriage was over and I was single again.

Mark was a widower. IS a widower. Horrible word. When we met we both knew the other had baggage. I didn't see it as a problem: you don't get into your forties without accumulating some kind of a past. Although I'd never intended to be anybody's stepmother nor had I ever harboured a desire to live abroad, I sold my apartment and we began the adventure two years ago: we bought a house in France. We're near the Pyrenees in the last bit of France before you get to Spain. Mountains, vineyards and Mediterranean beaches. What more could you want? Duncan came too. He looked chic in his new place; the tiles matched his little bronze eyes. Lucy would say that Duncan was very comfortable on his French hearth next to the Godin. He sat facing French doors to the garden, smiling his scaly dragon smile until three months ago when Liam broke him, swinging his school bag, he later admitted, as he walked past. Liam's thirteen now. He's supposed to be clumsy. I understand that. What I didn't like was the way he hid the piece of broken wing and positioned the fire dragon so you couldn't see the damage. Of course, next time I was cleaning, I discovered it and that's when it all came out.

"Leave it, Claire," Mark said to me, "I'll fix it."

"Why didn't you say something, Liam?" I said. "Why didn't you tell me?"

Liam treated me to one of his teenage shrugs. He kept his head down and his hair flopped over his eyes so I couldn't read his expression when he said, "I didn't know it was broken. I just picked it up and put it back."

Yeah, right, I thought, *and the broken pieces jumped up behind the clock on the shelf all by themselves.*

I suppose I should have said that aloud instead of thinking it but it's not easy being a stepmother. You have to watch what you say. I have a theory that stepkids get away with much more than other kids do just because stepparent is trying so damned hard to avoid the 'wicked' epithet.

Duncan took up residence in the garage on the workbench next to a pair of my sandals whose straps broke six months ago. Mark said he'd put a rivet through them, or something. We've a tap in the kitchen that squirts sideways, an electricity socket in the bedroom that hasn't worked since we got here and don't get me started about the washing line. They're all little things, small nuisances, but I could write a book about the number of times Mark has dashed off to help somebody else and neglected things needing his attention at home.

Liam's mother died when he was only three; he has no memories of her. Mark doesn't talk about her. It's as if the poor woman never existed. I look at the pair of them together sometimes and wonder what she would think if she could see them now. Would she be proud of her son? Of course she would. Any mother would be proud of the strapping lad who eats like he's hollow, is taller than me, who went to live in France with no French at all and is now so fluent his father relies on him to help sort out bills and taxes. And what would she think of Mark? Or did he always help to fit someone else's new bathroom while their own chipped and grotty sink needed ripping out?

Our neighbours in this small village think Mark's wonderful. They stop me in the village centre, at the paper shop or in the bakery to tell me.

"Oh, Madame," they say. "He is so 'gentil'. Nothing is too much trouble."

I smile at them and agree and think 'y*ou should see the obstacle course I have to negotiate to hang out the washing: unsteady piles of concrete blocks hiding potholes behind. You should see the gaps around the door frames where the winter wind comes blasting through. I put sellotape and duct tape round the windows to stop the draught last year. Have you got sellotape round your doors and windows, Madame? No, of course you haven't. Mark fixed your insulation last year, didn't he*?'

Winters are short but very cold here. They don't tell you that on 'A Place in the Sun'. I think Lucy forgot to tell Duncan, too. He couldn't live up to her promise. Houses are built with cold tiled floors in every room to keep cool in summer. That's when it feels wonderful to walk about the house with bare feet. You close the doors and windows to keep the hot air out and you pull the shutters tight to stop the sun destroying your furnishings. In winter, it's a different story. The Tramontane wind rushes over snow-capped peaks and stabs you in the back till your eyes water.

"Oh, but this is not so cold, Madame," they tell you. "It is much colder in England. Here, it is only the wind. Soon it will be spring again. See, the irises already have flower buds forming."

I'm too cold to go and have a look. And I want to say, '*Ah, but Madame, you are wrong about the weather in England. The thick clouds, which block the sun in summer are the same ones which keep the winters mild. And besides, Madame, we have things like central heating in England and fitted carpets which are soft and warm beneath your feet. Did you know, Madame, in an English house you can sit to watch winter television without an extra thick fleece on your back and a scarf around your neck?*'

Carpets and central heating are not priorities here and that brings me back to Mark's priorities, which is where I started and where I fit in with our odd family unit. Why did I move to France with Mark? Because I love him. At last, I had found a man I wanted to be with all the time. Why did I choose to be stepmother to an eleven-year-old? Because I love his dad. When I first saw the way they supported each other, how Mark was doing his best to be father and mother to his son, I dissolved. I was sure I'd grow to love Liam, too. He had to be a nice kid, didn't he with such an adorable father? Double helpings of niceness.

I send a cheque and a list to Lucy twice a year and we can get up to thirty kilos of goodies delivered from door to door for fifteen quid with an online company. Lucy loves shopping, bless her, and she goes out of her way to make sure we get the Brit things we miss. Christmas wouldn't be Christmas without your favourite sweeties and our best parcel of the festive season is the one with suet, for which there isn't a French word other than one that means 'grease', for making dumplings and roly poly puddings. Lucy packs everything in well: lazy gravy mixes, jars of Liam's favourite pickle, the one and only chocolate in a purple wrapper and digestive biscuits for the base of cheesecakes. She sends us pillows too, squashed up tight and rolled into a space-saving plastic bag with the air sucked out because French pillows are strange little square things like sofa cushions.

The winter parcel arrived this morning and Liam was hovering around, pretending not to be interested, but casting a sneaky glance while I unpacked the goodies and laid them out on the kitchen table ready for putting away. The table in the kitchen doubles up as worktop. It's a typical old-fashioned French kitchen with a tiny sink tucked into the corner and ancient cupboards with locks and keys. I thought it was quaint and cute at first. But there's nowhere to put anything down except the floor and the table. And then you have to shuffle things around in the cupboard so you know where everything is. I was on my knees on the floor with the parcel, sorting out packets and jars.

"Yay!" Liam said when he saw jars of Branston coming out of Lucy's bubble wrap. "Can I do some cheese on toast?"

"Good idea, Liam."

"Do you want some, Claire?"

I nearly choked. Liam offering to do something for me?

"Yes, thank you," I said. "I'm hungry."

"It's cold. We always feel hungrier when it's cold."

I nearly swallowed my tongue. Liam instigating a conversation? And using my own words?

Liam went for the cheese and I switched on the grill. We worked like a team and sat down together after we'd cleared a space on the table. I rolled the mobile paraffin heater closer. Liam offered me first dig in the pickle jar.

"Why didn't you and Dad get married before we came to France?" he said.

I did choke. I spluttered on my toast and had to cover my mouth. I looked at him. His face was composed, eyes alert and curious. "Well," he said. "It's a big move. Most people would want to get married first, wouldn't they?"

"Liam, I'm not sure that I'm comfortable discussing this with you."

"Why not? Got something to hide?"

He pulled a half smile and his eyes twinkled with mischief. He was using my own words again.

"So when did you suddenly get so grown up?" I said.

"Right after you taught me to do my own bacon sandwiches, cheese on toast and Spag Bol."

"Pity I didn't show you how to mend fire dragons," I said and flashed him a mischievous grin of my own.

"Dad wouldn't let me," he said.

"What?"

"He wouldn't let me have a go at fixing it. He said I'd make it worse. Said I needed steadier hands."

"Liam, when it comes to doing jobs around this house I'm sorry to say that your father's hands are so steady they don't even move."

He laughed at that and I felt a sudden urge to throw my arms around him and hug him but I reined in the way I've learned to do over the years.

"I'm sorry about Duncan," he said. "And I didn't really *hide* the broken bit. Well, I did, but it was only so I could mend it before you saw it. Then, well, you know the rest."

We finished our plates and I made us some coffee. I brought out the good stuff, one that brews in a cafetière and coats the inside of your mouth with a satisfying, roasted flavour. I love the smell of it. Liam was hovering again. I thought he was hanging around for something sweet.

"You could show me now," he said. "There's some glue in the garage. Dad's got all kinds of stuff in there." He brushed the flop of hair away from his eyes. He looked embarrassed.

"You're right. We've both waited long enough. Let's do it. Get your coat, Liam. And a hat. We're going in!"

The garage is a small barn where previous French owners would have kept their wine-growing machinery. It was freezing in there, the kind of cold that clings to your skin like a wet flannel. We bring logs in from under the overhang to dry out properly in the barn before we use them. I could smell them: a mixture of beech and oak, exotic like sweet and sour. They say a log fire warms you three times: once when you're cutting and stacking; once when you're barrowing them into the house and finally when you burn them. Apart from the paraffin stove in the kitchen it's the only source of heating we have.

"We'll get the log fire going while we're at it," I said. "Liam will you help me with the barrow?"

"Dad always lights the fire. He gets a bit, you know, funny whenever anybody else does his jobs."

"Tough," I said. "He's not here. It's cold. Liam, we're fixing the dragon AND we're having a fire."

It was nearly four in the afternoon. In the village centre below us lights gilded the cobbled Place as shops prepared for their second opening of the day. The sun had sunk below the hills. Purple shadows raced across the crags and gullies and the air temperature was dropping fast. My breath formed white mist around my face.

"Put some gloves on, Liam. You don't want to get splinters."

We stacked as much as the barrow would hold and wheeled it across the yard, crunching through the debris on the washing line obstacle course, to the house. We heaved the logs two at a time into the space by the burner in the living room.

"What about Duncan?" Liam asked.

"Blimey. Nearly forgot him. Poor Duncan. Hasn't had a warm backside in ages."

"I'll get him," Liam offered.

"And the glue," I shouted after him.

It takes over an hour for the sitting room to warm. I fasten the shutters closed and pull across heavy curtains to help keep out the draughts. The sellotape around the door and window frames rattles in the wind and every now and then makes a great buzzing noise like a child blowing through a blade of grass. The Godin is ticking, though, a comforting ping as the casing and flue begin to radiate. I throw on two more logs and stir up the hot embers.

Liam is watching television and I have my work on my lap, an illustration for a new book on Mediterranean gardens when Mark comes in at eight-thirty.

"I see you found the firelighters," he says, standing in the doorway. "Did you clear out the ashes first?"

I don't answer. We eat at seven. I put my Chinese brush in its stand and stare into the fire.

"We didn't need to, Dad. You don't have to do that every time."

I swallow my hurt pride, look up and say, "Everything go all right at the Ashfords'?"

"No. Does it ever? The walls are not straight."

"There's a surprise. French walls, not straight. Who knew?" I try to make the joke but I'm aware my laugh sounds forced.

Mark shrugs off his jacket and says, "I'm sorry I'm late. I had to stay to finish the job. You know the Ashfords can't afford to pay artisan prices. Hello! Duncan's back on his perch."

"I fixed him, Dad."

"*You* did?"

"It was easy. And I helped Claire bring in the logs." Liam holds out his hands under his father's nose. "Look," he says. "No splinters. No cuts. No broken bones. I'm still all in one piece. Ta-da!"

Mark's eyes fill. His mouth turns downwards and his cheeks flush. Liam stuffs his hands in his pockets and looks shame-faced and uncomfortable.

"Liam," I say, "Would you mind if I have a quiet word with your father? Could you give us a few minutes?"

"Sure. I've got homework to finish before Monday. I'll be in my room."

"No, sweetheart," I tell him. "It's too cold up there. You stay here. Your father and I will go into the kitchen."

I make some lazy packet sauce and pour it over the remnants of what had been a pork chop. Mark takes a seat at the table in silence, his eyes still gleaming with unbroken tears. I put down his plate and say,

"Why won't you let him grow up?"

"What?"

"You're holding him back. Why?"

"It's not like that," Mark says.

I sit beside him and say, "Well, what is it like then?"

"It's hard to explain."

"Try. You owe me that, at least."

He shifts in his seat and looks away.

"I promised his mother I'd always put him first. That I'd always be there for him. Take care of him, not let him come to any harm."

"Being there is what good dads do, Mark."

"Yes." He clams up tight as an oyster. His lips are drawn into an ugly thin line.

"Death bed promises," I say. "I don't like them. They're not fair on the people who have to carry on. What else did you promise?"

He can hardly speak; his sentences break into jagged fragments.

"I promised her . . when I found . . somebody else, she would have to . . . ."

"Have to what?"

"She . . . I . . would have to be certain that she really loved Liam."

It takes me a moment to assimilate what Mark has said. Then my stomach sinks. A cold void rips a hollow through my insides. I don't meet her criteria. The dead wife. The dead mother. The woman who never got to see her son grow up; the woman who never got to live in a house in France. Mark has chosen a new woman who doesn't know how to love children and here I am, enjoying another woman's dream, cooking for the lad with hollow legs, watching his shoulders broaden, listening to his voice deepen. Adult reasoning plummets into the black hole that has opened up inside me.

"If you don't want me here any longer, I'll go," I say.

"What are you talking about?"

"I'll go. Leave. You shouldn't make promises you can't keep."

"I don't know what I'm supposed to do, Claire."

"Wrong response, Mark. You're supposed to say something like 'but darling, I *love* you. Please don't go."

He hangs his head.

"You are allowed to love again," I say. "You know, that's the magic about love. It's fathomless. You can't measure it because it has no end. If you have a third child you love that child just as much as the first two, don't you? Love expands along with your capacity to give it. You don't have to steal from one to give to another."

He looks at me as if he's seeing me for the first time.

"We've never talked like this," he says. "We should have."

"I don't understand why that stops you from doing jobs around our house. It's Liam's home too."

"It's complicated."

"You don't say. Mark, we always knew our relationship was going to be complicated."

He rubs at his mouth as if more words are about to spill out of it and, afraid of their effect, he's trying to push them back in again.

"Before she was ill," he begins. "Before we knew how ill Jess was, I promised her a smart new kitchen."

Piercing cold again. Swirling up and out of the black hole, stabbing behind my eyes, scratching at my teeth and dry tongue, ringing in my ears making my jaw ache. Perhaps we should have talked like this long before. Maybe then I'd know how to cope with it now. A little frightened girl speaks in my place.

"So we can't have a new kitchen here because she never got hers. Is that what you're saying?"

He doubles up and crosses his arms across his body. Heat replaces the ice. The cold hollow turns in on itself and from somewhere deep inside me a rumbling, boiling storm of indignation rushes at my senses. I breathe in and out slowly to let the squall pass.

"Deal with it," I say. My voice comes out firm but soft. Little girl has run away. Claire is back. I'm not shouting. Not breathing fire. Can't release the anger scorching me only a moment before. Through our two years together I've never seen Mark look so vulnerable; he's always been so in control of himself, of what happens or not in the house, of Liam and,

I realise then, in control of me. I put my hand on his shoulder. "It's been ten years since she died. You have to deal with it. For Liam's sake. For your sake. Because you're both still here. It's not your fault that Jess isn't."

He nods.

"And it's not mine either," I add.

Liam comes into the kitchen wearing his hat and scarf and with his gloves on.

"We'll need more logs to keep the fire in overnight," he says. "Meteo France is forecasting sharp frost."

Mark stands up to go.

"I'm doing it, Dad," Liam says. "You finish your dinner. Belle-mère showed me how to stack."

Belle-mère, he's called me. Lovely description. So much kinder than stepmother. No heat burning me up. No ice cold hurt. Delicious warmth like cream and honey rises up and relaxes my face into a wide grin. I stand and hold out my arms for him expecting his usual rejection and casual shrug, but Liam throws his arms around me and lifts me off the floor. He swings me around and puts me back on my feet.

"Duncan's hungry," he says.

"I haven't got any cones, Liam."

"You have now. I found some in a candle shop." He hands over a paper bag. "I was going to save them for Christmas but I've just had a quiet word with Duncan and he tells me he can't wait till then." He winks at me and goes out to the barn for the logs.

Mark puts a match to a cinnamon cone and we wait around the hearth for Duncan's smoke. It rises in sweet wisps, curling out of his dragon's snout, sucked into the room by the draught from under the door. The glaze on his scales is chipped and you can see where the glue is holding broken pieces together. But he has a warm backside now and his favourite food in his belly. He's still smiling.

The Tenants

Nothing endures but change.
Heraclitus 540BC-480 BC

Her voice is like a sawmill. It slices the air. Its high pitch shrills and ricochets around the house. And it's loud. Always loud. She has only the one volume setting. The single variation in her speech is in the speed of her delivery: it gets faster when she's talking to the dog.

"Kenzo! Kenzo! Bring the ball to mummy. Allez. Bring the ball. Here, Kenzo. Ici. This way. Voila! Not that way. No, no, no. Here, Kenzo. Here, boy. Bring the ball."

Kenzo is a little dog with a yelp that's as high pitched as his mistress. He rushes on short legs at her commands and his yap makes him shudder all the way down his back to his stumpy tail. Faster and faster, her voice and his yapping gear up from strident overture into discordant symphony like screaming jet engines.

She talks to furniture, too. She talks to potted plants. She yells down the phone.

"There now," she shouts at the sofa after she's finished thumping cushions. "Isn't that better?" To the cushions she says, "And don't you look better, too?"

"Beautiful," she screeches at the agapanthus growing in pots by the gate. "You are so beautiful."

"Allo?" she shouts down the phone. "Allo? Benoit, is that you? When are you coming to see me? Good. Good." And Benoit has no choice but listen to her recount the events of her days as she calls out each detail, hardly stopping for breath.

In her early fifties at a guess, Gabrielle who lives alone is not unattractive. She's kept a slim figure and still wears a bikini when she's cleaning around the pool or sweeping away leaves fallen from shade trees out front. Two men come to stay over at weekends: not at the same time. One has a growl of a voice and grunts at night before he goes to sleep. He has huge hands and helps Gabrielle fix things around the house.

He would like to stay permanently but Gabrielle is not interested.

"No," she tells him. "I don't want a man around all the time. I have no intention of washing men's socks and underclothes ever again. I'm happy to see you every other weekend, Georges. We have a good time, don't we? Don't we, Kenzo?"

And Georges grimaces at the dog before he sits down to eat the breakfast Gabrielle has cooked for him.

The other one, Benoit, is a small man with delicate hands. He calls Kenzo baby doggy and coos at him. He likes to do the cooking when he visits. He takes Gabrielle out in his car and they always come back happy and smiling. Benoit doesn't ask to stay permanently. He has another life somewhere else, we think.

Gabrielle's hair is different shades of blonde, bleached by the sun a brassy yellow at the front and she wears it pulled back into a knot. There's always coloured polish on her fingers and toenails and she moves with some grace, it must be admitted. But the voice. Oh, the voice.

It never stops until she sleeps. Talking to the walls, talking to the table, talking to the dog and the sweeping brush, or whoever is on the phone, talking to the flowers, talking, talking. Too much. Too loud.

She cleans well, though. She polishes everything within an inch of its life, always talking to it, of course. She washes floors and wipes away spills. Gabrielle is practised in the art of the Mediterranean sweep.

We have a variety of winds here. There's one for every hour on the clock face or compass direction and they all have names. The *Cers* brings dust from the garrigue or flakes of charcoal from heath fires; the *Tramontane* and *Tarral* fetch grit from the mountains; the *Sirocco* dumps sand from the beaches. Then, the *Marin* brings rain and coastal fog and will leave a film of something that has to be hosed away if the Mediterranean sweep has not taken place regularly enough.

But Gabrielle is very regular. She likes her habits. Outside before eight o' clock she begins her daily routine, sweeping round plant pots, shifting outdoors furniture to get at dust underneath, talking to it as if it might see her and try to escape.

"Don't think I haven't seen you," she says. "Come here this minute and get in the dustpan."

Next door the English try to work out what she's saying. They call her Gabby and laugh when they say it. Perhaps the joke does not translate. The English talk quietly as if they are afraid someone might hear. Even when their visitors come they are careful not to make too much noise. They say things like,

"You must think about the neighbours," and they don't allow jumping in their pool.

Gabrielle takes a break from her cleaning mid-morning, has coffee and makes phone calls. Then she moves indoors and begins again. At the twelve o' clock bells she takes her light lunch outside and there is the briefest respite from her prattle but she drags her chair across the tiles so it screeches. Washing up takes place amid a clattering of ceramics and metal pans and cutlery while the radio blasts out popular songs and Kenzo yelps for scraps.

When Gabrielle has her afternoon siesta the neighbourhood relaxes. It's a *cul de sac* and used to be peaceful before Gabrielle arrived. When it was new it was the height of desirability. Villagers flocked to see the new show houses arranged around their own small Place. All different in design, they offered a new style of living far removed from dark three-storey buildings in the village centre that stand like sentinels around the church. Here, there are *chambres* on the ground floor with French windows opening onto the garden or terrace. You can step straight outside from the kitchen that has its own *buanderie*. Hanging washing is an easy affair. There are no steep steps to negotiate nor is there need for lines strung out across the street from house to house, or racks hanging from balconies

In the centre of the Place, where the road circles around a planting of cherry trees, there's a bench in the shade. Nobody ever uses it. It isn't the same as down in the village where residents use the benches daily to sit and exchange gossip. People here like their privacy. None of the neighbours comes out from behind their high walls and locked gates to speak to Gabrielle about the noise she makes. We think it might be the English who take this task upon themselves soon.

Before Gabrielle there was a family with a teenager out of work. She'd wander about listening to music or sit on a deck chair in the sun or sleep till noon. She bought sandwiches from the village shops for lunch and she left dirty plates and used cups everywhere. The father ran a tourist business at the coast, selling toys and trinkets, perfumed soap and tablecloths. His wife went with him in their white traders' van each day and they didn't return till late. Then, they'd eat and go to bed till the seven o'clock bells got them up for work again. There was no time for cleaning and looking after the pool. The daughter did nothing to help. Green slime grew on the water and on top of the used cups she left lying around; weeds poked through cracks in the paving around us.

We never bothered to learn their names. We were glad to see them leave at the end of the summer season.

Sometimes, there were even shorter lets: business people on secondment to another branch. We became a stepping stone on someone's ladder to success. They paid little attention to us. They were here, and then they were gone.

Sometimes there were families taking summer breaks. The children were allowed to run riot wherever they wanted. They smashed plant pots and broke the skimmer in the pool by jumping up and down on it. They smeared chocolate spread on walls inside and out; they scratched initials on the gate and stamped on lizards.

At other times there were professionals looking for work in the area. They didn't stay long. There's very little new work here unless it's attached to tourism.

We were temporary lodging, a transition between different phases of their lives, simply a convenience, no doubt forgotten as soon as they turned the corner on the day they left for the last time. None of the short lets cares about us. We don't belong to one another.

We miss the old man. Benjamin was here from the first and raised his family with us. He came to this village as a boy after the Spanish war and worked with his father in the vineyards. A handsome young man with bright eyes and a willingness to learn, he took after his mother and grew taller than his father. He had his mother's graceful build, her slender hands with long fingers. His was a gentle touch. When he spoke to us his voice was like a kiss, soft and warm.

Benjamin watched his father breaking his back over the work, out in all weathers, growing old and sick through the long hours and he determined on a better life when he was older. He worked hard, saved and kept his eye out for opportunities. By the time Benjamin married he'd bought land of his own and machinery to make the work easier.

He took some of us to his house in the village: a large *Maison de Vigneron*, built in the thirties when rail transport opened up markets further afield. There was no such thing as a motorway. The growers grew rich then. Houses grew grand. There were extra bedrooms and bathrooms and courtyard gardens where we stayed hidden behind wrought iron gates. Central heating had great metal radiators that clanked when they were warming up and cooling down. To the ground floor there was enormous garage space, big enough for tractors and trailers and tools and sacks of copper sulphate and insecticides. Outbuildings, big as barns, housed the vats and the presses and the bottling benches. There were close to sixty grand Maison de Vigneron in the village then, all with families producing their own labels to sell. People in northern climes had a liking for the taste of bottled sunshine: Languedoc rubies, precious as blood.

When competition made business harder the building of a co-operative facility introduced new cost-effectiveness but Benjamin saw a different opportunity. His Maison de Vigneron is now a Chambres d'Hôtes run by some people from Alsace offering travellers overnight accommodation and fruit juice and croissants in the mornings. The vats have gone to make way for visitors' garaging and in the *caveau* there's an enormous television screen and a table tennis set to one side. We heard there are television sets and computers in all the rooms and this is how visitors tire themselves. They work in air- conditioned buildings and come to the sun in summer for their annual break. They don't know what it's like to work through the heat till their clothes are wet with sweat and their skin is sore. They have no idea how savage the winds can be in winter when all the pruning is done by the hands of men bent double, frozen to the bone, with chapped fingers and gnarled faces. Holidaymakers are disappointed if they see a cloud.

Benjamin sold his vineyards to a development company and, when the Place was built, took first choice of the new villas, uprooted us from the village centre and brought us with him.

He was proud of his new modern home; even the garage had a place for everything. He pruned and he clipped; mended fence panels and unjammed gates. He built up his log pile and kept it dry and painted doors and shutters when harsh summer sun had stripped away the top layer. He was kind with us and he was kind with his people.

Madame Benjamin was a tender woman. She spoke gently to her children and kissed them often. She cleaned every bit as well as Gabrielle but without the constant noise. There was lavender soap in the bathrooms and spices in the kitchen. She cooked recipes her mother had taught her and grew herbs in a patch at the back of the house. She'd learned dishes from her husband's mother too so that the smells from the kitchen were sometimes from Spain and sometimes from France: paella with seafood and prawns, pieces of succulent chicken and mussels; cassoulet with juicy, fat pork and spicy sausages, beans and chick peas bubbling in rich juices.

Their children were courteous, serious types who studied hard to get to university. Monsieur Benjamin glowed with pride at each of their successes and pictures of them in their university hats and capes decorated the walls. The youngest, Céline found work in England and married an Englishman.

All three children offered Benjamin a home with them after Madame Benjamin passed away. But he chose to stay with us. He employed a gardener when his back grew too stiff. He would stand, not so tall now, beside the man and pass on his knowledge, demonstrating with withered arms and arthritic fingers how to hold the pruning shears at the correct angle.

When the English arrived next door he invited them in for aperitifs and when Céline brought her husband home Benjamin invited the English again to meet his foreign son-in-law. He brought out Madame Benjamin's best faïence serving dishes with dainty biscuits and spreads, tapenades and olives as he knew she would have done. He sat smiling as they conversed in his living room although he understood not a word. His face lit up as he listened to them speak in English and pride shone from his eyes every time Céline translated for him.

Through the long lonely summers, when the temperatures soared, he took an early morning dip even though he was in his eighties by then. He cooked meals his wife had cooked and seemed content to live out the rest of his life with us.

Every spring he went to stay with the daughter in Aix, and because he thought it proper when visiting Provence, he would wear all white. He'd put on his white linen suit with a white shirt and a creamy white tie and on his head a white flat cap with a little peak to keep the sun out of his eyes. The English would wave him off and say,

"Safe journey, Monsieur Benjamin. We'll keep an eye on the house."

And then, one spring, he didn't come back. Benjamin's daughter came to collect his things. She went to see the English to tell them about his passing and how we would be let until the rest of the family had decided what to do about us.

So now we have Gabrielle and she takes care of us in her own way. She keeps down the weeds. But it's not the same. Everything is changing. Behind our Place another vineyard has gone to make way for housing. The first parcels of land have already sold and the houses they are building are shoddy affairs, too small and too close together. They have no outdoor space: nowhere to grow things. They spoil the view we once had over a vast expanse of us, rolling in stripes toward the hills where the sun sets.

Gabrielle chats to the people who come to see how the building work is getting along.

"Yes, it's a lovely village," she tells them. "And so friendly. From the Pays-Bas, are you? You won't have any problems here. Stop that, Kenzo. We have English and Irish and people like yourselves, and the odd German, many from Spain. I said, stop that, Kenzo. Kenzo, go inside. Allez. Allez."

Her voice follows its usual pattern, rising through the octaves, a crescendo of sawing discord, and when the Dutch people have left she tells Kenzo all about Holland.

"Kenzo," she says, "we didn't know you looked like a Smoushond, did we? Fancy that! You are a little Dutch dog and your cousins are the Schnauzers from Germany. We shall all be safe from the rats and mice as long as you're around, Kenzo. Sweet little Kenzo. Would you like a biscuit, darling? Here we are, then. Kenzo! Stop that, Kenzo."

No, we don't belong to one another, Gabrielle and us. We were the first lost vineyard and brought new life into our community. There was hope in the beginning. A little growth was meant to help increase revenue, keep the village thriving. But, like canker, the growth hasn't stopped. A scourge is creeping.

We miss the quiet days when the men came to test the soil. We miss the dark nights full of silent stars and the smell of the earth. We ache to feel the wind rattling our branches and singing through the wires, and the leathery sound of bats that flew over us from the church tower, cigales drumming in the trees along the lanes by day, crickets chirping by night.

We yearn for the sharp bite of a February frost, the warm rain of summer, the salty tang of southern breezes. We long to hear the rustlings of small creatures hiding from red kites, circling and staring down, hanging in blue sky above, and the shrill crack of October rifles among the red and gold of our autumn foliage and the dogs snuffling along the rows.

We miss the gentle voices of the men at their tasks, their friendly chatter as they found shade beneath an olive tree and sat to eat their lunch baguettes and cheese.

We long for the touch of the careful hand that knows where to cut, the soft whisper of his breath against our skins. We miss the old man.

The Silent Movie Star

Confidence is the sexiest thing a woman can have.
Aimee Mullins 1975 -

Her arrival was perfection. As the crush of glitterati moved toward the entrance doors and hungry photographers scanned the red carpet for that last, biggest scoop, the 1930 Packard Speedster slid up beside the kerb. Elegant as the swan on its hood the vintage car glided to an aloof halt, meticulously positioned between two rows of barriers holding back the crowd. A polished chrome entrance if ever he saw one, fascinating as a slowly creeping glacier.

All around him cameras flashed at the Packard's gleaming white bodywork. Noisy photographers scrambled for position, elbowing each other, lenses trained on the Packard's rear passenger door.

Which remained closed.

The clamour stilled. Onlookers whispered.

"Who is it?"

He didn't know either. He looked at his notes. An impressive guest list but who was still to come? Behind him the last group of A-Listers paused to see the cause of the sudden hush. The women turned away again and went inside. But the men stayed to stare at the fabulous car. Someone touched his shoulder. A familiar Scottish burr said,

"Who is it?"

"I don't know."

"Ach, I just got to find out."

"But aren't you with . . .?"

"She can wait. I just got to see *this*."

Even legends in their own lifetime couldn't resist a mystery, he thought. The most famous 007 ever stood beside him, drooling to see who was going to alight from that closed rear door. One didn't name names. And to have to ask would be an insult. These people should need no introduction. Even if, up close, their complexions were not quite as flawless or line free, even if the recent, deliberate weight loss had given them a sallow cast, the hair colour was overdue a touch up or the hair itself not as luxuriantly thick. Real stars needed no introduction. You never gushed in the presence of stardom. You mixed with the royalty of the silver screen as if it were an everyday occurrence and kept the stars out of your own eyes.

The Packard chauffeur got out and adjusted his hat. He stood to one side of the rear door. The crowd waited, necks craned, eyes pinned. He pulled open the door and stood to attention. The interior of the car was dark and, it seemed, occupied only by shadows.

Another quiet wait.

Cameras poised.

People holding their breath in the cool night air.

Slowly, a black silk leg emerged veiled by metres of narrow pleats, the foot barely visible in its silver and diamante high heel. He scribbled in his notebook.

Slowly another leg appeared.

She unfurled from her seat like a sleek black cat in bugle beads and stood aside as her chauffeur reached inside the car to retrieve her purse. He handed over her cigarette holder into her gloved hand and she struck a pose, one leg of her palazzo pants slightly in front, shoulders back, head tilted to one side, chin barely raised. Frantically he checked his guest list again.

Her eyes were amazing: huge and dark. They flashed myriad messages:

At the crowd, her eyes said, *I'm so pleased to see you.*

At the leading men waiting by the entrance, *Call yourselves actors?*

And when she caught sight of him standing on the red carpet with his microphone, the silent challenge of her faint smile that didn't reach those glittering eyes hit him like a slap in the face.

He'd seen the style of her outfit before somewhere, the long strings of black and white pearls, the silver tasselled scarf around her head wound into twists and plaits. The matte, red mouth. What was she? Twenty? Thirty? More? He couldn't be sure. Worse, how was he going to address her if he didn't know who she was? He stepped forward and approached. His steps were short and careful, his hands outstretched in greeting.

"Good evening," he said. "May I take your invitation?"

She turned her back on him and struck another pose for the cameras, biting at the tip of her cigarette holder. "Madam," he said. "May I take . . ."

Again she ignored him. He turned to look at the doorman who shrugged.

"Leave this to me," said 007 offering the woman his arm. Without acknowledgement of either the actor or himself she linked arms and, in a waft of exotic perfume, the couple drifted past him, past the door staff and on, through the entrance and out of sight.

***

He caught up with 007 at the champagne bar.

"What did she tell you?" he asked as the music segued out of the theme to *Star Wars* and into *Pirates of the Caribbean*.

"Nothing."

"Nothing?"

"A big, fat zero."

"So, we still don't know who she is."

"No. Damned annoying. Everybody's talking about her."

"What are they saying?"

"Same as us. Wondering who she is. Why she won't speak."

"You mean she hasn't spoken to *anybody*?"

"Not a soul."

The music slid into the theme from *Mission Impossible*.

They stood together and watched her moving through the room. She held the long cigarette holder in one gloved hand, a glass of champagne in the other. She moved with grace, languid as a contented panther. One by one, other guests stood back to let her pass. He saw how they couldn't take their eyes off her. Sometimes she smiled at them; sometimes she turned away. But the red lips stayed pressed in their tight pout.

She put down her empty glass and moved on from group to group. She came close enough for him to see the flash from those dark eyes, the dismissive flick of her wrist as she let people know she'd finished with them. She was icier than the ice sculpture on the top table.

"She's up for an award, isn't she?" 007 said.

"Looks like it."

Never had he witnessed anybody make such an impression by saying nothing at all. The silent woman in black silk had every male pair of eyes turned in her direction. But, *who was she*?

It was almost time for the award ceremony. Maybe he could find a way to get her to speak to him. He could try flattery or he could pretend he didn't care who she was. Sometimes indifference worked better. He picked up two glasses of bubbly and took one to her.

In the subdued lighting her skin seemed to have light of its own, like the pearls at her throat. As he drew closer her perfume filled his senses. She smelled of green things and dark chocolate, soft *and* strong, and another scent that lingered after the others had taken their effect. His head was in a spin; he'd forgotten what he was going to say. Silently, he offered her a glass. She accepted with a smile and clinked bowls with him. He cleared his throat and found his voice.

"They tell me you're not speaking to anybody," he said.

She nodded. The tassels on her silver scarf flickered. Dark chocolate, spring flowers, summer fields and autumn forests wafted around him. He breathed them in. "Not speaking to anybody. Staying silent all night long. Is there a reason for that?"

She brought her hand to her chest and grasped at her sequinned top as if she was afraid. Then, she lowered her head and stared at the floor. When she looked up again her eyes were dewy. Her brow was in tight knots. Pain dripped from her velvet-clothed fingers. Misery wracked her shoulders. A single tear rolled down her cheek. Her back arched in silent agony.

Shock dried his mouth. Once again, he could hardly speak. He ran his tongue across his teeth.

"I get it now," he said. "You're a *Silent* Movie Star. Darling, you're fantastic."

***

She looked like his wife again minus the scarf, the high arched eyebrows and ebony contact lenses. He watched her getting out of their car and wanted to pull her close.

"Come on," she said. "Let's get all this stuff put away. We'll tidy it up properly tomorrow."

They stuffed the red carpet into their garage, went indoors and turned up the heating.

"I think they had a good night," she said. "We gave them some magic, didn't we?"

"They're probably still talking about it. You did a fantastic job with the venue, darling. Just like the real thing, but I thought you said you weren't coming to this one."

"All part of my plan, hun."

He poured them nightcaps. Wanted to hurry her to bed. She wanted to toast another successful party night.

"Rent-a-crowd did us proud tonight. Don't you think? That was a great turnout," she said.

"Probably because of whose party it was. Anyway, it works every time. Put a few professional looking guys with cameras outside and passers- by always stop for a nosey."

"So what did you think of my arrival?" she said.

"I didn't recognise you at all," he said and stroked her hair.

"Good. That's what I wanted. Did all their guests turn up?"

"All but four. I hope they've got a good reason. Old 007 will be after them when they get back to work."

He moved toward the stairs. She followed him, but still wanted to talk.

"I think you made the right decision awarding best costume to the little Harry Potter," she said. "How old was he?"

"Only twelve. 007's grandson, sweetheart. Had to be done. We picked up another three bookings tonight," he said. "Two more Hollywood themes, and a Sci-Fi night. But don't go splashing out on fancy hire cars like that again."

"No. It was a one-off. Shame though. I liked it."

"Mind you," he said. "I liked your outfit. You haven't thrown the contact lenses away, have you?"

"Why, what's on your mind?"

He sidled up beside her and kissed her neck.

"That perfume," he said. "It's new isn't it?"

"You would have recognised my usual one," she said and kissed him back.

"Let's go to bed," he said. "And put on the dark eyes. I've never made love to a Silent Movie Star before."

"Sweetheart," she said. "You've had Marilyn Monroe, Tinkerbelle, Lara Croft, Jessica Rabbit and countless others."

"I know, I know. But this one's more mysterious."

"Well," she said. "I can't promise to keep quiet."

Tom's 2010 Cruise

Behind every great fortune there is a crime.
Honoré de Balzac 1799-1850

Tom Ramsbottom's invitation to sit at the captain's table came two nights out from Venice. Meticulous in his preparation for the event he checked in the full-length mirror, turning to view every angle of his hired suit. He had to bend carefully to tie the laces of his dress shoes, needed to wedge himself against the wardrobe door to keep his balance against the pitch and roll. He took special care with the bow tie. He'd never worn one before.

He straightened up and stretched his back; jutted his chin and twisted his neck around to ease the starchy crispness of the stiff shirt collar. He glanced again at the luxury cabin. Fresh fruit compliments of the management overflowed from a lavish basket on the sideboard. Creamy thick carpet cushioned the floor; soft lights pooled from hidden recesses around the walls. He grinned at his reflection. He smoothed back the grey hair at his temples and ran his tongue over his teeth.

"Bloody Hell, Tom," he said. "Captain's bloody table, no less. Bugger me."

Cocktails for the select group were served at six-thirty in the Milano bar and restaurant, the premier dining suite on the upper deck. Tom hadn't met any of the other guests and stood alone, admiring the clean lines of the chrome and glass décor, the high polish on the pale sycamore bar fittings. The Captain approached him and they shook hands.

"Signor Ramseybottome, forgive my Engleesh. Is not sound good. Welcome to Donatello's. Your first time with us. Yes?"

'That's right, Captain."

"Is good here for you? Yes?"

"Oh, yes. Thank you."

"We are small cruise company. Not like packed with people. You understand me? Small groups. Is more pleasant."

Tom nodded.

"Is more relaxing."

Tom added a smile to the next nod.

The Captain lowered his voice and narrowed his eyes: "Is more exclusive."

Is more bloody expensive too, Tom thought. Less than a third the usual number of passengers, more than twice the price. They'd never believe this lot, down at the Rose and Crown. Donatello's. Tom Ramsbottom, drinking G and T in the Milano bar, cruising down the Adriatic with Donatello's. *Bloody Hell.*

The Captain moved off to greet the others and Tom was by himself again. Nobody else sought him out to make his acquaintance. He thought about making an approach but changed his mind when the lady looked straight through him and turned her back with a flounce. The draped fabric across the shoulders of her evening gown fluffed out in a floating aura of pale grey as she twisted away from him. He thought her over-theatrical. He watched as she smoothed the narrow pleats back into place then ran a slender, bejewelled hand over her sleek hairstyle.

At the dining table he found himself seated between that same lady and another. He smiled and nodded politely to both of them as he took his place. Old girls, they were, now that he could see close-up. Maybe even a bit older than him. It wasn't their faces; it was the leathered chests and the backs of their hands that gave them away. Their faces had been pulled tight against the ravages of time; more than once, he guessed.

There was something vaguely familiar about the face that belonged to the boyish haircut and pale grey pleats. It would come to him. The one on his left spoke across the table to the distinguished-looking man opposite her. Her husband, Tom gathered. Tom drew in his chin and looked away; she was too loud and made him feel uncomfortable.

"I do hope the weather improves soon," she said. "One doesn't expect grey skies at this time of the year."

"I'm sure it will," the man replied.

"The thing is, one can't quite decide what to wear."

"I'm sure you will," he said.

"Tomorrow, for example," she went on, her voice growing louder. "When we go onshore. I should like to lunch at that charming little *ristorante* under the giant oleanders. You remember?"

"I'm sure we will," he said and picked up his fork.

The lady sniffed and began, delicately, to sample the melon *chiffonade*. Tom waited for the woman in grey on his right, took note of which cutlery she selected and followed suit. He took a stab at the Parma ham.

He glanced quickly around the table. It didn't seem to matter to any of the others that they were chewing on uncooked bacon. His tongue probed to dislodge a piece that had glued itself to his palate. He was glad he'd got his new bridge in.

"Signor Ramseybottome," the Captain called from around the table. "You 'ave met Lady Somerton?" He indicated the old girl in grey on Tom's right, the one who had ignored him earlier. "Of the world-famous Somerton fashion house?"

"Good evening, Lady," Tom said.

She turned her coiffed head towards him and looked surprised.

"Somerton!" she added.

"I'm Tom," he said. "Tom Ramsbottom. From Bingley. In Yorkshire. You might have read about me in the papers."

Her lips pursed in a peculiar lopsided curl. "I don't take the News of the World," she said with a sigh and turned away from him again. He wanted to say more but decided against.

The *I'm sure* man leaned forward to catch Tom's eye.

"Charles," he said, holding out his hand across the table. "Charles Forster. Pleased to meet you, Tom. Sounds like you've got a story. In the papers, eh? What'd you do?"

Tom put his hand inside his jacket and brought out a carefully folded news clipping. He handed it over under the chilly gaze of the two women beside him.

The waiter came to clear. Charles Forster leaned sideways, unfolding the paper. When the next course arrived over his left shoulder he sat hidden behind a page of the Daily Mail.

"Charles," his wife stage- whispered. "Your scallops!"

"Bugger the scallops," Charles answered through the news- sheet.

Tom chewed the inside of his cheek to avoid laughing. He waited as Charles read. From opposite sides of the class-divide, they were, but it didn't matter. Here was a man Tom could get on with.

Charles refolded the page and handed it back to Tom. He scooped up a portion of the St Jacques and swallowed.

"Too much garlic," he announced to the table. "So, Tom. This is quite fascinating. Tell me more. How did you come up with the idea in the first place?"

"Well, it's like this. I've got a good memory."

On the half-moon stage, backed by a twinkling starry curtain, the six-piece orchestra began with the theme from The Godfather.

"Bugger!" Charles said. "I can't hear you now, Tom." He pointed to his hearing aid. "Got to turn this thing down. Too much background noise makes the bloody thing whistle."

Tom nodded his understanding.

"See you in the bar later, Tom. Good man."

Tom was about to reply when he was interrupted by a loud, insistent beeping noise. The Captain consulted his pager. He scanned the read-out and frowned. He stood.

"Please to excuse me," he said. "I come back. Soon, I hope."

Nobody spoke through the sorbet. Tom enjoyed letting it melt slowly in his mouth. He scanned the room. It was like one of those films Kath used to enjoy of a Sunday afternoon, all gloss and glitter. After roast beef and Kath's Yorkshire puddings they'd take their apple pie and custard and eat it in front of the telly. She loved those old Hollywood musicals. Poor Kath. She'd have been out of her depth with this lot here, now.

Halfway through Chicken Marengo and Lara's theme from Dr Zhivago, the Captain returned to the dining room but walked to the stage and took a microphone. The orchestra stopped playing. The lights came up. Silver plate clattered against porcelain as the diners lay down their cutlery. The Captain cleared his throat and looked directly across at Tom's table.

"Signor Forster, ladies and gentlemen," he began. "There is change. The weather is not good. Is getting much worse. I make decision to divert. We are 'aving permission to make way to Isole Tremiti. There is good safe harbour there. More details later. I thank you very much."

The Captain regained his seat at the table and immediately fell into conversation with Charles. The others waited patiently, Tom noticed.

"How long do you anticipate?" Charles asked.

"Is 'ard to say, Signor. These storms, they come quick and sometimes they go quick."

"But sometimes they last for the best part of two days," Charles added.

The Captain lowered his eyes. "Is true," he said. "We must wait. Is all we can do."

"Wait where? San Domino?"

"Si, Signor."

"Send the entertainments manager to see me after dinner. I'll take my coffee in the bar."

"Si, Signor."

Two cups of espresso arrived as Tom and Charles settled into leather club chairs in a quiet corner of the bar.

"Something strong to go with that?" Charles asked. He turned to the waiter. "Bring my bottle of Hine Antique, will you?"

Charles poured large measures. Tom took a sip and licked his lips.

"Like it?" Charles said with a smile.

"By the livin' daylights! That's grand. It's like cream. Soft. Smooth. You the big cheese round here, then?"

Charles nodded while he swirled cognac around in his mouth.

"What are you doing as one of the passengers?" Tom asked, taking another taste.

"Sampling," Charles said. "Like Sir Richard. You never know when he might show up on a Virgin Atlantic flight. I like to see first-hand what's going on. Meet a few satisfied customers. You know the thing."

Tom leaned back as far as the chair-design allowed. His rump slid forwards on the leather and he pushed himself upright again. Charles screwed up his eyes.

"You're absolutely right, Tom," he said. "These chairs are damned uncomfortable. Look nice, and all that. But not what a man needs for his comfort. Must do something about that. Good man."

Charles slipped his hand into his breast pocket and brought out a miniature Dictaphone.

"Club chairs," he said into it and put it away. "So, Tom. Back to the newspaper story. I'm listening. You said you've got a good memory."

"I have. I never forget a fact. Not once I've learned it properly."

"Such as?"

"Inventions. Who invented what. Sporting records, Grand National winners. That kind of thing."

Charles sat bolt upright. "1987?"

"Maori Venture."

"88?"

"Rhyme 'N' Reason."

"Red Rum's three wins."

"Too easy, Charles. 73, 74 and 77."

"A harder one, then." Charles sat with his hand across his chin, pushing his lips together between his thumb and forefinger. He leaned forward. "1963."

"Ayala, owned by Mr Raymond- Teasy-Weasy hairdresser bloke," Tom said, and something else clicked into place.

"Ha!" Charles slapped the table and the glasses chinked. "So how did the good memory help you with the car competition?"

Tom winked and tapped his temple.

"Well now, I remembered when Ford launched their new model in the nineties. They'd been designing since 1986 and the thing that was different was that the design and marketing was shared by Ford USA and Ford Europe. Over six billion dollars, it cost. One of the most expensive programmes ever. They wanted a car for the world, took the French word for it and added an 'o'. Simple. Monde became *Mondeo*. I used the same kind of thinking."

"Bloody marvellous," Charles said. "Go on."

"So, I think to myself. Italian manufacturer. Hybrid-fuelled engine. Need something a bit futuristic, like."

Charles nodded.

"Well, I'd just taken the grandson to the cinema, hadn't I? We both loved it. Avatar. Have you seen it? You should. Anyway, so everybody's talking about the film and I read about this car competition. I remembered the Ford story and stuck an 'i' on the end of Avatar. *Avatari*. Futuristic-sounding, don't you think? Comes from Sanskrit, you know. I looked it up on the internet but I think it sounds Italian. Perfect. There's one waiting for me to pick up when I get home."

Charles put down his glass. "And this trip was part of the prize?"

"That's about the size of it."

"Excellent. Bloody marvellous. Fancy a cigar?"

"Inside?"

Charles snorted. "Bugger the EU," he said.

A thin man in casual wear and carrying a briefcase approached the table. Tom saw the apprehensive look in the man's eyes, the crease in his forehead, the slight stoop of his shoulders.

"Ah, Dominic," Charles said. "Pull up a chair. Drink? I think you know why I wanted to have this little chat."

Dominic, the entertainments manager, bit his lip and scrunched his forehead.

"I'll think of something," he offered.

"We'll need a few ideas from you if this weather continues. One shore trip will kill an afternoon but there's not much in the way of sightseeing in San Domino. Especially in a squall. Indoor activities. That's what we need." Charles leaned back, waiting for a response.

Dominic brought out a pad. He sat with his legs crossed, tapping his pen against his cheek and looking at the ceiling. Tom watched him crossing and uncrossing his legs. The pen tapped against the notepad. The gaze moved from the ceiling to the walls. The legs uncrossed and the toes of Dominic's shoes tapped together. The pen knocked against his teeth. Tom watched till he could stand it no longer.

"I'll do you a quiz," he said.

***

"A quiz?" Lady Somerton sneered as she read the bulletin posted on the entertainment notice board. She turned to face the small group who had gathered at the entrance to the breakfast room. "Do you suppose they mean as in a 'Pub Quiz'? How extraordinary!"

"Have you been outside this morning?" Charles Forster's wife said. "The weather's appalling. I think the best thing to do is curl up with a book. We shan't be going anywhere for some time."

"But, really, Anna. A quiz? Isn't there a church or something on this island that we could visit? A museum, a gallery? I mean, really. A quiz?"

A tall man, standing at the back of the group, joined the conversation.

"I'm up for it," he said. "Come on, ladies. Join in. Could be fun."

Lady Somerton drew herself up and breathed in hard through a pinched, upturned nose.

"I really don't think so," she said. "There must be something better to pass the time."

She pulled her signature, silver grey pashmina around her shoulders and stepped away. Her route back to her cabin took her past the computer room. Charles Forster almost bumped into her as he came out onto the inner deck.

"Lady Somerton. Good morning. I hope you slept well. Not too much bouncing around once we'd made harbour, was there? Breakfasted, my dear? Good." He leaned back into the computer room. "Bloody marvellous, Tom. Can't wait. I'll make sure Dominic gets you a good crowd."

He turned back to face a stiff expression and cold eyes. "What a memory! Never forgets a fact," he said and strode off.

Tom got up and came to the door. Lady Somerton continued on her way.

"What's the rush?" Tom called after her.

She kept a firm gaze ahead.

"It's rude to ignore people, Connie," Tom added.

The interruption in her stride was barely perceptible.

"You don't want to have this conversation out here in the open, do you?" he said.

She stopped and turned towards him.

"There isn't going to be a conversation," she said. "I have nothing to say to you."

"Not coming to the quiz, then?"

Her mouth curled like before.

"Funny you should mention The News of the World, last night," he continued. "Only, I'm putting a few questions in the quiz that you might be interested in."

She looked at him from under half-closed lids.

"You are sadly mistaken," she said.

Tom took a step towards her.

"I know I'm not. I never forget a face either, Connie."

"Someone told you my name. What a foolish game this is."

He moved in close beside her and lowered his voice.

"Here, listen. Remember the Profumo affair?"

She brought her hand to her throat.

She took a seat beside him, as if they were working together on the PC.

"You'll pardon me for saying this," Tom said, "but if you'd grown older, shall we say, naturally, I might not have recognised you at all."

She pulled on a piece of hair at the back of her neck and looked at the floor.

"Get on with it," she said.

"Nineteen sixty-three, Connie. 1963. Just after the Profumo business. Do you remember we had a little scandal of our own in our neck of the woods? All over the Yorkshire Post, it was. Wealthy landowner and the barmaid. Ring any bells? You came out of it all right, though, as I recall. Married the old boy, didn't you? Good move, that, Connie. You got lucky there, I think."

She shifted in her seat and took a deep breath, releasing it slowly, as if she was bored.

"Popped his clogs five years later. Left you his fortune. Good for you. Used it to set up the frock business, did you? Nasty court case though, his kids contesting the will."

"I married well. What's so unusual about that, these days?" She stood up to leave. "You are a thoroughly disagreeable little man. What on earth do you hope to gain by attacking me like this?"

"That's an interesting question, Lady. Did you know I used to be a plumber's mate? Did the rounds servicing central heating boilers. Got called out at some strange times. Especially up to The Grange. You know, before the old bloke died."

Her hand went to her neck again and she sat back down in a hurry.

"My boss was doing quite a lot of a very different kind of servicing. We used to call you Lady Chatterley behind your back. Well, you've got the same name, Connie."

He saw a flicker of embarrassment cross her face.

Tom continued. "Do you remember, Connie, you had a cleaning lady called Kath?"

She shrugged. "I never used their first names. How would I know if one was called Kath?"

"Kath Wilkinson, she used to be, till we got married."

She sighed. "Oh, for Heaven's sake. Now, if that's all you have to say . . ."

"Sit still, Connie. I'm not finished. You need to hear this."

Tom closed the door. He stood beside her with his hand on the back of her chair.

"You fired Kath the first time she had a bit of morning sickness and was late for work. You wouldn't get away with treating people like that nowadays, Connie. I said, sit still. I haven't finished. We had a little girl," he said. "Our Carol. She's grown up now with a little boy of her own."

"How nice for you." She rolled her eyes.

"Look at me, Connie when I'm talking to you. Don't sit there, staring into space."

Reluctantly, she turned her head to look at him. He took her hand and held onto it as he watched her face.

"I want to say something to you. Thank you," he said.

"You what?" She pulled her hand away.

"See now, that's how you used to speak. None of this *Good Heavens* and posh lah-de-dah stuff. You used to be one of us. But I don't blame you for getting on in the world. I want to thank you."

"What for?"

He stuffed his hands in his pockets and rocked on his heels.

"For putting me and Kath together. While you were entertaining my boss Kath used to give me a cuppa and a slice of cake. We'd sit in your kitchen and just talk, like. She's been gone two years now."

He leaned forward and patted the bejewelled hand.

"But if it hadn't been for you, Connie, if it hadn't been for your carrying on with the hired help, I might never have met the love of my life. So, I say thank you for being who and what you are."

The door to the computer room burst open. Charles came in.

"Need a hand, Tom? Hello? You two look pretty serious. Something the matter?"

Tom was aware that her body stiffened. Her face paled and her hands clenched. Frightened eyes begged him. Her reputation was his to do with as he wished. He had the power to ruin her but the thought of it, the satisfaction that she knew it too was enough. He leaned over her and clicked the mouse.

"Lady Somerton wondered how to set up an account on Facebook. Just the thing for keeping up with all your old friends. Don't you think so, Charles?" he said.

"Wouldn't have a clue, Tom. Wouldn't have a clue."

Charles threw his arm around Tom's shoulder.

"Let's have a look, Tom. Never could fathom the attraction of those chatroom things."

Charles scratched his head as Tom took his students through a quick demonstration.

"You know, Tom," Charles said. "You've just come up with another idea for an indoor activity. Teaching dullards like me how to do this. I don't suppose you'd fancy a nice little summer job? What do you think, Constance?"

Lady Somerton opened her mouth but nothing came out.

"No thanks," Tom said. "I wouldn't want to be away from my grandson for the whole of the summer. School holidays, you see."

Charles clicked his fingers. "No problem. You could bring him along."

"He's too young for this kind of thing, Charles. You're very kind, but . ."

"Alternate weeks?"

Tom smiled. "I can see you're used to negotiating, Charles. But, you know, you can't negotiate with someone who doesn't want to play his part in it. I've got my life and I enjoy it. What would they do without the quizmaster at the Rose and Crown?"

"Fair enough." Charles relented. His eyes lit up and he grinned. "Tom, I've got another one for you. Mr Teasy-Weasy. Raymond Bessone. What was the name of his other Grand National winner?"

Tom laughed. "You can't catch me out. It's what I do best." He winked at Connie in her House of Somerton silver and grey ensemble and quietly he enjoyed the irony of the correct answer. "Rag Trade. 1976," he said with a knowing nod.

What Time is it Mr Wolf?

Beware of a wolf in sheep's clothing
Aesop c.620-564 B.C.

I'd developed such a crush on him. His messages were savvy, smart, clever. A little bit sassy but not too much.

"Be careful," my friend, Morag said when I first told her about him. "You can't believe everything he's telling you."

"I am being careful, but, you know what? I'm tired of being careful. I want to have a life."

She pulled that face meaning *don't say I didn't warn you* and I just grinned and shrugged my shoulders.

"Julia, *sweetie*," she said. "You're such a target for these online predators. Look at you. Ten months single and raring to go."

"Predators?" I said. "That's a bit strong."

"Well some of them are, you know. They probably message all the females to see who's easiest to get at. I've heard it's like Albert Square on Eastenders at some of these free dating websites. They've all had each other already and pounce on new members straight away to see who can get in there first."

"You make it sound like a competition."

"Well . . . for some of these types maybe it is."

"They can't all be like that."

"Julia, I'm just saying be careful, that's all. Look, let's take a break. I need food."

Morag has been divorced for longer than I have. She has a couple of male friends but nothing serious. She says she's not interested in washing socks and ironing shirts ever again. We were hitting the Saturday department stores, shopping for cosmetics. She wanted to top up her usual brand. I was looking for something different. A new face for the office at the college where I work and an evening face for something more glamorous. Since moving on with my life I'd begun to take more interest in fashion, makeup and hairstyles. I felt as if I needed to experiment with reinventing myself to find out who I really was. And the truth is, I *had* forgotten who I was. I'd been a wife; I was still a mother. Now the children were grown and off leading their own lives and the husband had disappeared into the sunset with his new love interest. So where did that leave me?

I didn't want to spend the rest of my life as a single woman. Not that I can't function on my own. I manage very well. I have a reasonable income and a good group of friends. I have the freedom to go where I want, when I want. But having that one important, special person in my life is important to me.

I missed having a man. I missed the pleasures of a warm, loving and intimate relationship. It's funny how quickly I stopped missing my ex, though. I'd reached a point where I didn't think about him at all. He was out of my life and, since our children are adults now, there was little reason to need to contact him about anything. But was I really ready to meet someone else? Sometimes the thought of actually, you know, doing it filled me with dread. Could I cope with intimate knowledge of another man's body? How would I feel at the touch of another man's skin? Might even a kiss turn me right off?

Morag led the way into the self service restaurant. I could smell fries and onions and pastry. My stomach gurgled and I realised I was hungry too.

"Come on," she said. "If we're quick we'll beat the lunchtime rush."

She was right. As soon as we found a table and put down our trays, the place filled. The queue tailed right back into the furniture department. Then the buzz of voices and clattering of cutlery grew louder. I reached for the ketchup.

"So," she said, settling into her seat and raising her voice above the clamour. "What's his name?"

I leaned forward so I didn't have to say it loudly. "His profile name is Lumière. His real name is Michael."

"You've got as far as real names then. Lumière? You mean like that candlestick in the Disney film? Have you seen a photo of him?"

"Yes."

"And?"

"He's very handsome."

She pursed her lips and put her head on one side in that *knowing* way. "Spanish looking. Dark looks. Dark eyes. Just your type." Her eyes challenged me.

"I know what you're going to say next. He looks nothing like Ian. Michael isn't as tall for one thing and he has that beard fashion going on."

"What? How old is he? I thought beards were for much younger men."

"Well, he is a bit younger than me."

"A bit." She put down her fork and stared at me. "How much of a bit?"

"Ten years."

I waited for a lecture. I couldn't read her face. She remained silent for a moment. Then,

"Describe him to me."

"Oh, he's kind of a mix between D'Artagnan and Aramis." My stomach fluttered at the thought.

"A Musketeer?"

"Sort of."

"Lucky you," she said and gave a little laugh.

"Maybe. I don't know yet."

"Sweetie," she said, her voice all kind and gentle. "He could be a breaker of hearts. You don't need that right now. Promise me you'll be careful."

I was a complete novice at this online dating malarkey. Think of it, a woman my age exchanging witty banter with a complete stranger, a man who could be lying through his teeth about his background, his work. Perhaps lying about his reasons for being a member of a dating site. Morag could be right. Michael, Lumière Musketeer could be a serial cheat, a *predator*.

After a few weeks of messaging we exchanged email addresses and telephone numbers. I wanted to hear his voice. It had never occurred to me how important a person's voice is when you're getting to know them. When all you have to go on are written messages it's as if part of their personality is missing. What if he had a high-pitched, girly voice? Supposing it turned out he really was a lovely, sincere man that I could fall for and then his voice became a deal-breaker. I was longing to hear what he sounded like.

And he called. Fates have mercy on me, he could do voiceovers. You would buy whatever he was selling. He did a voiceover on me, that's for sure. I swear if I hadn't been sitting down I would have swooned. His voice was deep and rich and smooth, like dark chocolate. I would have stayed up all night just listening to him. He seemed sincere about wanting to meet me and, like a schoolgirl, I felt my stomach give a little flip of excitement. He said he'd call again soon to make arrangements.

I walked on air for days, filled with the promise of wonderful things to come. During quiet times at the office and at home alone I imagined how it would be when finally Michael and I stood facing one another. How one thing would lead to another. Oh, Lordy, my body reacted. I wanted him. I really wanted him.

I arranged to meet Morag for a drink after work on Friday two weeks later. Our local village pub is a welcoming place. There's a pretty garden out the back for warm summer evenings and indoors two open log fires at each end of the long bar make for cosy winter nights. I know many of the regulars and I feel quite comfortable going in on my own. I arrived first and ordered at the bar. A bottle of red. Morag and I leave our cars in the car park at the side and walk home afterwards.

"You've changed your hair. I like it," the barman said. "Going on somewhere nice?"

"Thanks, Rob. I'm meeting Morag. She'll be here soon."

"Somebody should snap you up real soon looking like that," he said and winked.

"Cheeky!"

Rob must be all of nineteen years old, younger than my son. But a bit of flattery felt incredibly welcome. When Morag arrived I ordered a soft drink while she caught up on the Merlot.

"Sorry I'm late," she said, slipping off her jacket and sliding onto the bench seat by the window. "All hell broke loose this afternoon in A & E. Had to call security and everything. I had to write up a report. Oh, I'm ready for this." She took a large gulp. "How are you? You must be feeling disappointed."

I nodded. "Yes, I was disappointed when he never called back."

"Scoundrel," she said. "He was playing a game with you, sweetie."

"I know that now."

"They should kick them off the decent sites. There must be plenty of dating sites that are all about illicit relationships. Having a bit on the side in secret. Look at that case a while back in the papers."

"But Michael wasn't after an illicit relationship, Morag. Was he?"

"He must have been. Why all the secrecy? Why let you think one thing when he had other intentions?"

"There was no secrecy. He told me his real name. He has his photo up on the site. He gave me his real mobile number and email address."

She laughed. Took another drink. "Oh, Julia," she said. "He probably has dozens of different email addresses and several mobile phones, one of which is for his dating contacts only. You were such an easy target, darling."

"I know."

"I'm sorry it didn't work out for you. Anyway, you might have gone off him in any case, once you'd . . . you know. He was probably contacting lots of women at the same time, working out his options. He should change his profile name to Heathrow." She laughed again.

"How do you mean?"

"Stacking women in a holding pattern like planes waiting to land."

"Maybe. It doesn't matter."

"Oh, I know now why he uses Lumière for his profile name," she said, throwing back her head and laughing louder. "It means light, doesn't it? He likes attracting women like moths to his flame. He was no better than any other wolf, sweetie. Pretending to be something he isn't. So he has a nice face and a sexy voice. He has a way with words. But that's it. That's all there is. I bet his messages were conspicuous by their absence at weekends. Were they? Did he ever contact you at weekend?"

"No."

"What does that tell you? Busy with his real life at weekends, Julia. Probably a wife in the background who knows nothing about what he gets up to after she's gone to bed weekdays." She was on a roll. I watched her getting heated on my behalf. "It was a game. Not a very nice game, was it? He'll get what he deserves treating people like that. There's somebody better waiting for you. Don't be sad. Be angry."

I wasn't sure Morag would understand my real feelings. I wasn't sad, nor was I angry. So I told her how I felt.

"Actually, I'm grateful to him."

She nearly choked on her drink. "Grateful? How can you say you're grateful?"

"Yes. I am. I've learned a lot thanks to him."

"What? Learned that the world is full of lying, cheating rats?"

"No. I learned enough about myself to know I'm really ready to move on. I was excited about him. I was really looking forward to finding out more about him. I even got to the daydreaming stage." I lowered my voice. "I was even imagining making love with him."

She smiled and nodded.

"I know what you mean," she said. "Been there and done that."

"Well," I went on, " I wanted it. I knew I would like it. Before Michael I didn't know whether I would ever feel like that again. Didn't know if I *could*. Now I know I can."

"And that's enough to make you happy?"

"For now, yes."

And I'm content. Ready to move on with my life. Thanks to a wolf in sheep's clothing I know I'm ready to open my heart to the right man when he comes along. It's time. It's a good feeling.

Lost Dreams

Dreams are today's answers to tomorrow's questions.
Edgar Cayce 1877-1945

I have a book about dreams. It's thicker than a family bible. It sits on a lower shelf on the bookcase by the front door. The spine is faded from where sunlight catches it but the front cover is like on a fantasy novel. There's this beautiful young maiden reposing on misty clouds surrounded by all manner of weird and wonderful creatures guarding her while she sleeps. It's a very girly illustration, romanticised to the point of absurdity. Nobody looks that lovely when they're asleep.

The book tells you what dreams are supposed to mean. I think somebody who believed in all that stuff once gave it to me. For example, if you dream of being in a fairground it's symbolic of life's ups and downs. And if you dream of plumbing, *as if*, what you are doing is looking at the way you direct your emotions.

I'd think, *no, really? What a load of codswallop.*

The dream book nestles between *Nature Through the Seasons in Colour* and *Everyday Life through the Ages*. They've been on that shelf for years They're all dusty. I keep promising myself I'll have a clear out but I never get on with it.

There are always other things to do, more important issues, more pressing. Dusty bookshelves don't amount to much when there are emergencies that can't wait. Every day, it seems, there are more and more of these things that can't wait. There is always an endless queue of urgent to-do's demanding attention. It's like constant firefighting. All the time you're occupied putting out one blaze there's some idiot somewhere whose sole purpose in life is to light more fires to get in your way. Life gets too full of targets and deadlines. It's exhausting. Who has time to dream?

I know I'm in bed. I can feel it all around me. It's been another busy day and I really need to go back to sleep. If I don't get my full night's sleep I know I'll feel ragged at work tomorrow. We've got a visit from the Divisional Superintendent. Mister Hedges. Master of the comb over and Acqua di Giorgio. Incongruous mix. Nice smell; bad hair.

I need to be sharp. Got to have my wits about me. I must have figures memorised. I'll be expected to answer all his questions in depth. But I mustn't think about that now. I need more sleep. I should relax. Stop thinking about work. Concentrate on something else. The pillow is soft and cool beneath my head. Please let me go back to sleep, I say, but not out loud.

There's someone in the bed beside me. I know who it is, of course. It's him who's always there. You know. The other half. I can feel the warmth from his body in the bed beside me. It's comforting knowing this person so well who shares our bed.

But there's a face keeps appearing in my mind. It's another man's face and I know him well, too. Wait a minute. Stop this. How come I'm in bed here with Mr Comfortable but in my thinking there's a handsome face that won't go away?

I like the way that bit of hair curls on Mister Lovely's forehead and I've always admired the shape of that mouth. He's telling me something and I know what it is without hearing his words. I'm planning to go somewhere with Lovely Face. Are we going to run away? He's smiling at me and encouraging me to come away with him.

What? Now? In the middle of the night?

I'm grinning in the dark.

I want to. Oh, I really want to.

But, I can't leave Mr Comfortable. I love him.

And Mr Lovely Face says, but you love me too.

I put on the kettle for coffee. My eyelids are heavy and my head's in a fuzz. There's a pain in my shoulders as if I've been scrunched up all night. I stretch my neck and attempt to uncurl. I can feel tissue and bone grinding. I'd really like to go back to bed and sleep some more but I have to leave the house in fifteen minutes for work and the meeting with the Divisional Superintendent. Jack has already left. He has a full day ahead of him too. He won't be back till very late and then he'll eat and fall asleep in front of the television.

I run through figures, mentally chanting them the way I learned multiplication tables as a schoolgirl in list form to help me remember. I throw a cereal bar into my handbag. There's no time to put up a packed lunch. I'll have to eat in the canteen today. If I can fit it in. If the superintendent clears off before lunch is finished. I check in my purse for enough cash.

Yes. I have enough coin. Good. I wouldn't have time to go to the bank machine on the way in to work. You'd think they'd take debit cards in the canteen, but, no, it has to be cash. They have to balance the till and deliver the takings to the general office each day. I don't know why. Here's a five pound note in my purse, too. I unfold it and slip it into a pouch. There's a photograph in the wallet side of my purse. I look at it. My heart thumps.

Where did you go? I say. *When did you turn into Mr Comfortable? Oh, Jack Lovely Face, I miss you.*

There's a heavy feeling in the pit of my stomach like a hard, sour lump. It must be nerves. It's because of the Superintendent's visit, I tell myself. Only, I know that's not the reason. I'm used to visits from the higher-ups descending on us, trying to catch us out.

Yes, Mr Hedges, the new line is selling well. Here are the figures.

No, Mr Hedges, we returned that faulty consignment to the manufacturer.

No. This feeling in my stomach is like a kind of stage fright. Nervous and anxious. As if I was getting ready to go on holiday and worried I might have forgotten something. What is it I feel I have lost?

Sales figures and percentages are still streaming through my thoughts like a matrix of never-ending data. I can see them in my mind's eye, scrolling down the screen in my head, month by month. Ten week forward estimates; current percentage increases. Targets met; targets missed and reasons why:

Terrible weather that weekend, Mr Hedges.

There was the opening of that new supermarket across town.

Special offers from the competition.

I check my bag again. I need a new pack of handbag tissues. Sometimes when I'm talking about my work I end up with lipstick on my teeth. Maybe I talk too fast. Well, if I do it's only because there's so much you have to squeeze in so the higher-ups can see you're on the ball. You want them to notice you're on your toes. You want them to say,

Nothing gets past you, does it Mrs Williams? Oh, Mrs Williams, is that lipstick on your teeth?

That was embarrassing. I won't let it happen again. So, I always keep tissues handy. Just in case.

That must be what I'd forgotten. That'll be why I'm on edge. I haven't lost anything. I'm anxious because I don't want the lipstick thing to happen again. I just need tissues. I keep some on the bookshelf in the hall. Here they are above that dream book.

Dreams, I say. *Who has time to dream?*

And then it hits me. What it is making me feel anxious.

The thing I have lost.

It's Lovely Face. He's gone away and I can't find him. Why has he gone away and left me?

I reach out to take a pack of tissues, but the voice in my head won't stop.

You used to have time to dream, it says. *You used to make time for Lovely Face and dream with him.*

Cold rushes at me. The back of my neck tingles. I stand there staring at the title on the faded spine of that old book and the truth is like an icy slap in the face.

Lovely Face is still here. He's always been here. Right beside you. It's <u>you</u> who got lost.

I don't want to listen. Haven't got time to listen. I stuff the pack of tissues into my handbag and rush back into the kitchen to gulp down the last of my coffee. But the voice follows me.

It's you who got lost, it repeats.

I shove my used cup in the dishwasher. I check the time. I should leave now but there's something I have to do first. I know it's going to make me a few minutes late but I have to do this *now*.

I go back to the bookshelf and take down the dusty dream book. With a tissue from the pack I dust it. The colours on the front cover are fresh as new. The reclining maiden's dress is jewel bright. It falls in luscious folds from her spangled belt, floating in a twinkling aura around her cloud bed till it becomes stars in the night sky. Her hair gleams in silver moonlight as it tumbles over her cloud pillow. I flick the pages and sniff the paper. It reminds me of a perfume I used to wear years ago when I had a passion for ethnic clothes and essential oils. As she lies there, sleeping in the clouds, the fantasy maiden looks peaceful. She's smiling as if she's enjoying her dream.

And now I've done what I came to do. I must put the book back, put it to rest. It's just a book. I tell myself dreams are just dreams. I suppose, though, it would at least be *useful* to be able to make sense of them. If such a thing were possible.

Hello, the voice says. *Don't you remember thinking that once before?*

Who, me? I don't think so.

You were curious.

Me? No, never.

You had an open mind then.

It's nonsense.

But my fingers have a mind of their own. I'm still holding onto the dream book. I haven't let go. I look down at the book in my hands. I let the pages fall open wherever they will. I read the page.

And I know it doesn't matter what it says. It's not important which page has fallen open. I sense the message would be the same on every page.

You have lost who you used to be.

I rush to the door. There's no time to think about it all now. It's only a dusty book. I'll sort it out later.

In my car I'm on auto-pilot driving through a morning shower. I don't remember passing the filling station and the pub on the corner, but here I am at the traffic lights waiting for them to turn green. On amber the sun breaks through and the road ahead shimmers. The fantasy maiden's hair is cascading over cars and buses in the queue. Road signs and shop fronts are spangled stars spilling from her skirts. The pavements are sapphire skies below her cloud bed.

Another flash of truth jolts me. I *am* the dream book. My colours are all still there underneath but they've been hidden from view. Jammed tight on a dark shelf between other forgotten things. Not getting to see the light.

It's green now. Time to go. Time to move on. I've never felt so certain of what comes next. This coming weekend there's nothing more important than Jack and me. I'm going to reintroduce Mister Comfortable to Lovely Face and we'll take it from there. Maybe Mrs Busy can rediscover her own neglected Happy Face.

I remember now who gave me that book.

I did.

14 Tweet story

"Dance like the photo's not being tagged, Love like you've never been unfriended, Tweet like nobody's following." - @PostSecret

Tweets are short messages on Twitter. They must be no more than 140 characters long which includes spaces. The following is a flash fiction piece I Tweeted to my followers.

1. When he got up he didn't notice anything different. She looked as if she was still asleep.
2. He had work to do. First, the sink to bleach; he liked the smell of it and *she* never did it properly. Then, his phone calls.
3. He made coffee. Went outdoors. The day was set fine. He'd be able to get those seedlings planted out.
4. He smiled, having the day to himself with no interference. Retirement meant doing exactly as he pleased. He'd earned the right.
5. At twelve he began to feel hungry. He wondered, briefly, what she was planning for lunch but there was still no sign of her.
6. He looked in the fridge and grabbed a crab stick. It wouldn't spoil his appetite for later. There was no sound from the bedroom.
7. His stomach rumbled as he opened the bedroom door. He called her name. Her face was pale and still. Grey and unattractive.
8. He thought about the greyness of her. There was no wonder he hadn't wanted to kiss any of it in years.
9. He made tea and enjoyed rearranging the caddies and repositioning cups in better places in the cupboard on the wall.

10. He spent the afternoon lining up plant pots. He finished the crab sticks. He thought her selfish not making him refreshment.

11. At seven, when he wanted his dinner, he realised she was dead. Brain haemorrhage, the doctor said. Ah well, he thought.

12. How could he have known she was dead? Why would any man make it part of his morning ritual to check if his partner was alive?

13. She'd done it on purpose, of course. To make him look bad.

14. Ah, well. Now she'd got everything she wanted. She'd often told him she felt she was dying inside.

THE END

Airport Departures

There is no remedy for love but to love more
Henry David Thoreau 1817-1862

I notice the child first. She looks about seven or eight years old, a slim, pretty little thing with dark hair pulled into a twisted knot on top of her head and tied with pink ribbon. In her candy striped tights, she is hopping from one dainty foot to the other.

"Papa," I hear her say. "I need pee-pee."

A tall man takes her hand and leads her away, she skipping along, Papa dragging hand luggage behind him and juggling boarding cards and passports. The departure lounge at Montpellier is full; the queue for the ladies' disappears around the snack bar. I lose sight of them and return to my book.

But, I can't concentrate. I read the same sentence three times. The girl has reminded me of my granddaughter when she was that age. The same questioning eyes, the same perky nose. A pang of nostalgia stabs me. How quickly the years have flown. I look up from my book and search for the mother.

Where is the mother? My stomach flips. Wouldn't the mother be the obvious one to take the little girl to the toilet? Why do I suddenly feel afraid?

Two seats against the near wall are occupied by a large doll and a child's hand luggage, the kind that is usually stuffed with colouring books and crayons. Two seats. Not three.

Where is the mother? I close my book and wait.

I hear the child coming back to her seat. Her singsong voice flies ahead of her. Her shoes tap on the tiled floor. Then, she appears from around the corner by the snack bar.

"Mademoiselle Effie," she trills. "Don't cry. I am here." She picks up the doll and comforts it, patting its bottom and kissing its face. "Look, Papa. Effie has been a good girl." She holds up the doll to be kissed. "Papa! Effie wants you to kiss her."

The child's French is beautifully pronounced and rounded. Not acquired in this part of the country, I decide, where vowel sounds are short and hard. Her little mouth moves with the sounds of her mother tongue and is as pouty as a French girl's mouth ought to be.

"Papa," she says again, pushing the doll's face up to him.

He bends and plants a peck on the doll's face. She sighs and cradles the doll in her arms, gazing down upon it from under thick lashes. Oh, she has her father's eyes, dark as night.

He is a handsome man with a strong nose and firm chin. He would be in his mid forties, I think. A wonderful age when men are at their most manly, it seems to me. Why is this handsome man travelling alone with his daughter? My stomach flips again and I fear for them. What family tragedy lurks behind their brave faces?

But the child is happy. She fidgets and fusses over her charge. She straightens the doll's clothes and smooths its hair. She shuffles and shifts in her seat all the while talking to Effie the doll. Up on its feet one minute, on its back on the child's lap the next. Then its front. The woman in the seat next to the girl flinches as the doll's head barely misses her face.

"Josette," her father says. "That's enough. Watch what you're doing. Sit still."

In shock I bring my hand to my mouth and I look away quickly patting the back of my hair, pretending a little cough, hoping nobody has noticed.

Josette's father is *English*, his accent one with which I am familiar. A man from the north of the country if ever I heard one. I had assumed he was French. But those are the clipped vowel sounds of a Yorkshireman. So, what is their story, this handsome man and his beautiful young daughter?

My gaze drifts back into their direction. I try not to let it be too obvious. I wonder if there are other people in the departure lounge thinking along the same lines as me and I glance around. No. It's only me. Being curious. Being nosy, maybe. Everybody else is minding their own business: busy sorting papers and documents; finding cash to buy drinks; reading.

I hold up my book in front of my face, every now and then peeping sideways at the objects of my curiosity. Papa is a strong, manly man from the north of England. Josette, his little daughter is as French as French can be. Like the rest of us in the tiny departure lounge they're booked on a flight to Leeds/Bradford airport. And the mother is missing.

Josette asks for a drink. Her father zips open his hand luggage and produces a small carton of juice.

Ah, I think, he's very well prepared. Did he think of that himself? Has he got a bag full of things she might need? Did someone else pack that bag? Might it be the mother?

Josette accepts the drink and tears off the drinking straw attached to the side of the carton. She slurps her way through all of it and hands back the empty.

"Josette," father says in English. "Go and throw it away."

"You do it." This, also in English with the poutiest of French pouts. "I have to stay with Effie."

"You can take her with you."

Those pretty eyes scowl and the mouth twists. But, father is having none of it.

"Josette. Throw your own rubbish away."

I want to smile at him, let him know I understand and approve.

None of my business. Look away.

But Josette has answered her father in *his* mother tongue. With *his* Yorkshire accent. Delightful.

She must have spent enough time with her father to develop that northern accent. Oh, please don't let them be another broken family.

I board the aircraft before Josette and her father. I'd paid extra for priority boarding; it gives me a little more time to get up those steep flights of steps and into my seat. I always board at the rear entrance now. The stairs to the front of the cabin give me nightmares of stumbling on the extra deep, steep steps and causing the whole queue behind me to fall like a row of dominoes.

All through the flight I imagine Josette's story. Her father has flown from Yorkshire to France to collect his daughter and take her home for the French spring holiday. Somewhere there would be a grandmother like me, longing to see her grandchild, aching to make up for lost time. Worse, for him, the handsome father, time only to catch up on his daughter's progress at school, her latest interests and so on before it would be time to take her back to her mother.

I turn to the window. Puffball clouds float below us, drifting by like my thoughts . . .

You can never make up for lost time. It's gone forever. The years cheat you into thinking there's plenty of time stretching lazily ahead and then, before you know it, your grandchildren are no longer small. They are teenagers and don't want to be treated like children. They don't do hugs so readily any more.

I have two grandchildren, both teenagers now. Once, on a visit to see them in England when my grandson, Tom was six he had forgotten who I am.

"I'm your mummy's mother," I reminded him. I smiled but the pain was sharp. It brought a lump to my throat that my dear little *petit fils* had got himself all mixed up because he knew people usually had two grandmas. Therefore, I couldn't possibly be another one. Besides, I was a foreigner with a funny voice. Was I his aunt, he wondered? Afterwards, he apologised so politely the pain of my love for him misted my eyes.

But this is what happens in broken families. The grandma who lives furthest away is replaced by grandfather's wife. In my case, grandfather and the new grandma lived in the next street to the grandchildren. No amount of phone calls from abroad can make up for that kind of daily contact and when the novelty of Skype or FaceTime wears off youngsters haven't got time to have half an hour with you before bedtime. They're out to swimming club or rugby till half past nine or later and then it's too late by the time they get home.

You are not a *real* grandma. Real grandmas baby sat for years and were there, on hand to help out in emergencies or collect the kids from school. Grandmas who live abroad, like me, are grandmothers in name only. We wear the title like an honorary degree but we haven't worked for it. Haven't *earned* it. Parcels and presents from an absent grandmother don't match days at the seaside, regular walks with the dog by the river and bedtime stories by a winter fire. Those are the little things you can never make up for no matter how hard you try.

I married an Englishman. We first met when I was on an exchange visit with my college and stayed with the family next door to Stuart. Then we met again at university, married and had a daughter, my only child.

My husband was unfaithful for years. In the end I couldn't cope with it and divorced him but stayed nearby so Emma still had contact with her father. Stuart and I got along in a reasonable fashion, keeping polite, not saying nasty things about one another. He had a lot of girlfriends and then, quite suddenly, decided he wanted to settle down again just when our daughter had her own marriage plans. They were married on the same day. Emma wed her David in our local Parish church; Stuart went for the ceremony plus honeymoon on a Caribbean beach. Emma couldn't forgive him for the longest time for not being there to give her away. She asked *grandpère* to take her father's place. He came to the wedding alone, my mother was too ill to travel.

When my mother died I returned to France to take care of papa. I had no idea at the time how long I would be away. I always intended to return. I rented out my house in England rather than sell so that I would have a place to come home to one day.

I think that's when it all began to fall apart. I wasn't there when my grandchildren were born. *She* was, though, Karen, Stuart's wife, the replacement grandmother. She stepped into the breach, filled my role and Emma forgave her father.

I could see how things were going to develop as soon as I made my first trip back to visit my new grandchild. I had to sit in the back of Stuart's car, of course. I was a passenger, a visitor. On the way to the hospital the conversation was all about the night of the birth and how, if it hadn't been for Karen's quick thinking, newborn Lauren might have arrived in the back of a taxi. Karen had been the heroine of the day, insisting they went to hospital when my daughter said she still had plenty of time. Karen took my place on that day and kept it ever afterwards.

Soon, we are flying over the Channel. With just over half an hour of the flight remaining, I see Josette making her way to the toilets at the back of the cabin. It's her second trip in forty minutes.

Too many cartons of juice?

I used to sit in the cinema when Emma was little wondering why she was making her second trip to the toilets in a similar short time. I never did get to the bottom of her fascination for using all the conveniences wherever we were whether or not she needed to. And the step thing. She couldn't pass a flight of steps without running up and down them. Garden paths, store entrances, doorsteps and the like.

Hold on a minute, Mum, she'd say, *just let me . . .*

And then her own daughter, my *petite fille,* Lauren had the same little obsession. Toilets and steps. Steps and toilets.

And now, here is Josette doing just the same thing. My stomach knots.

Oh, please don't let them be another broken family.

We come through arrivals close together. Josette and her father are just ahead of me. They walk toward a woman, about my age, waiting at the barrier.

Look at her face. I know that feeling. She's holding out her arms and Josette is running . . .

Hands come from behind me. Long fingers over my eyes. *Ma petite fille!*

I peel back the fingers and see Emma in front of me, grinning. I spin to greet Lauren and I hug her hard. Then, the three of us embrace.

"Where is he?" I say. "Where is my little . . .?"

"I'm here, Grandma."

It can't be possible. In the five months since I last saw him my grandson has shot upwards. He is looking *down* on me. I can't believe how grown up he looks. He's finally overtaken his sister and is looking down over the top of her head too.

"Tom," I say. "That can't be you. Emma, what have you been feeding him?"

He shrugs his shoulders and takes my bag. I notice how long his strides have become as he leads off through the airport terminal. An image of fat, bent and awkward toddler legs makes me smile as I remember how he used to have a funny, rolling gait when he first learned to walk. Now, he is striding out like a man. Or is it just that I am getting much slower?

On the journey from the airport everybody talks at once. The nervous knot in my stomach unravels itself and I relax into chatter about computers and social websites and who is going out with who. David is away at a business meeting but will be home the next day. Tom carries my bag up to my room for me and Emma and I open a bottle of wine before preparing the evening meal.

"I have something to tell you," Emma says.

"It sounds serious," I say, gauging the tone of her voice and the anxious look in her eyes. "Go on."

"David has a promotion."

"That's wonderful news."

"It means we'll have to move house."

"Well, that's exciting, isn't it?"

"To Cambridge."

"Lovely."

"Cambridge, Massachusetts."

"Ah."

I look at Tom and Lauren. They are smiling, their eyes bright and excited.

"We'll be going to the International College. It looks fantastic," Lauren says. She brings up an image of the new college on her tablet and shows me, with some pride, where they will be attending classes. A neo-classical building surrounded by Italianate gardens and fountains, the college appears a prestigious place to study.

"So what's the problem?" I say.

"What makes you think there's a problem?" Emma asks.

"I can tell."

Emma puts down her glass.

"It's Karen," she says. "She's become very clingy and morose."

"She doesn't want you to leave. Is that it?"

"I think so."

We speak later in more detail when Lauren and Tom are occupied in their rooms.

"Karen is going to pieces," Emma tells me over after dinner coffee. "She says she can't bear to be without us."

Now here is a strange situation: my daughter asking my advice about how to cope with her stepmother. Deep inside me a nasty little voice is saying,

Aha! Now, Karen, you're finally beginning to understand how I have felt all these years.

Instead, I say, "What can I do to help?"

Karen is conspicuous by her absence that night. The phone is noticeably silent. On previous visits I'd been used to several interruptions from her. She would always telephone with some piece of information for Emma that was apparently too urgent to keep waiting, or she would come to the house bearing sweets and gifts for Tom and Lauren. It went on for years. She could never allow me time with my grandchildren alone, it seemed to me and, at first, it made me angry that she would continually find ways to interrupt. Now, I understand her fear.

"Ring her," I suggest. "Invite her and your father to dinner this weekend. I'll cook."

My time with my daughter and her family runs out too quickly, the way it always does. We watch favourite films and cook favourite meals. The evening with Stuart and Karen goes well until the last half hour.

"What do *you* think about them all going to America?" Karen asks me once Tom and Lauren have gone upstairs.

"I think it will be a wonderful adventure for them," I say.

Out of the corner of my eye, I see Emma wince.

"Well, it's all right for you," Karen says. "You're used to not being close. You haven't been there for them every day, the way I have. You've been apart from them all the time. You're used to it."

"You never get used to it," I say quietly. "It's a pain that never goes away."

She brings out a tissue and sniffles into it.

"I don't want them to go," she says.

"I know," I say. "I understand. Try to be happy for them. It's what *they* want that matters, isn't it?"

"Oh, I see," she says, her voice growing louder. "It's all about self, is it? Doing what you want and blow everybody else's feelings? Like mother like daughter?"

"Karen!" Stuart says. "What do you think you're doing?"

"There comes a time when you have to step back and let them move on without you," I say, looking directly at Karen. "It is very painful, but it is the right thing to do."

Emma and David have left the room. I can hear them in the kitchen, talking in low voices.

"I think it's time we went home," Stuart says and takes hold of Karen's arm.

I don't say any more. I've said enough. Karen will have to find her own way through it. I pop my head into the kitchen and ask if Emma wants me to help but they've already cleared. I go to my room to pack for the morning's flight. I can hear Karen and Stuart outside by the garden path saying goodnight.

"See you tomorrow," Karen is saying. I don't hear her apologise for her outburst.

Packing to go back home is always an easier task than when you're choosing what to take away with you. I roll up my things and tuck them into my cabin bag. I don't know when I'm going to see my English family again. I'm zipping up my bag when there's a knock on the door. Tom comes in. Lauren follows.

"We'd like to come and stay with you," Tom says.

"For a holiday," Lauren adds.

"What does your mother say?" I ask.

"She thinks it's a great idea. We were going to wait and surprise you with it later but Mum said to tell you now."

"Well, that's just wonderful," I say. "When would you like to come?"

Emma is standing in the doorway, peering through the space between her children.

"For the summer?" she says.

I flop onto the bed. I know I'm grinning fit to burst but my legs have gone wobbly.

"David and I have a lot to sort out before we go," Emma is saying. "We're planning to leave during the six week summer holiday. Can you have them for me? Tom and Lauren would like it very much."

Could I have them?

Of course it's all right with me.

"What about Karen?" I ask. "Won't she be put out?"

"Mum, leave that to me."

By the time Tom and Lauren are leaving the house for school on Monday morning I have my bag ready and waiting by the front door. David has left for the office. Emma had an early dentist appointment and has already left the house. Stuart gives me a lift to the airport. I sit in the front of his car, the first time that has happened in years.

"Thank you for offering to run me to the airport," I say.

"No trouble at all," he says. "And thank you, too."

"What for?"

He shifts a little in his seat and looks uncomfortable.

"Helping Karen," he says eventually.

"I didn't know I had."

"I think she needed to have things put in perspective."

I don't know what to say to him. He has no idea how difficult it had been not to shout at her. He hasn't a clue how I'd wanted to scream at the top of my voice to tell her how lucky she'd been to have Lauren and Tom all to herself for most of their childhood. Stuart would be shocked to learn how for years it seemed to me neither he nor Karen cared very much how I was feeling when I became an outsider in my daughter's life.

Stuart pulls into the drop-off zone and lifts out my bag for me. He takes hold of my arms and kisses me on the cheek.

"I probably won't see you again, will I?" he says.

"Probably not," I agree. "I'll be flying trans Atlantic from now on."

"Karen is afraid of flying."

"Ah."

I wave and walk into departures. My steps are light, my head buzzing with plans for a whole summer with my grandchildren in south of France sunshine. I sail through security and on into the shopping area. I haven't bought treats for myself from duty free in ages. I browse and choose a favourite perfume.

"Effie!" a little voice calls. "Come here this minute."

I spin around and there she is, dragging the doll behind her. My stomach sinks. Josette's hair is hanging loose and untidy. She looks bedraggled. Her little cardigan is buttoned up lopsided and the hem on her skirt has come loose. I can hardly bear to look up and see her father's face. I know the expression he will be wearing. I wear it myself every time I come away from my visits. Except for today. This time I have something exciting to look forward to.

Josette's father is sitting in the waiting area reading a newspaper.

He's keeping himself occupied. He's burying his face behind that newspaper so she can't see the pain in his eyes. He's taking Josette back to her mother. A long weekend with his daughter is all he's had.

Another broken family.

I choose a place to sit where I can't see them. Selfishly, I don't want their pain intruding on my happiness. I pretend to be busy reorganising my bag, finding a better place for the duty free carrier, rearranging things and slotting in my English newspaper. Doing everything I can think of to keep my mind on Lauren and Tom and the joyous weeks ahead. Anything rather than witness Josette's father's suffering.

I board the plane from the back and take a seat next to the window where I can close my eyes and ignore Josette's trips to the toilets.

I must have dozed. The *fasten your seat belt* light pings and rouses me. I can feel the aircraft making its descent. I glance out the window and see the coastline below us. I recognise beach resorts east of Montpellier. I watch buildings grow closer and then make out flamingoes on the salt marsh.

Home. Plans to make. My grandchildren all to myself for six whole weeks!

As I wander through passport control toward the arrivals hall I'm thinking about museums and trips to the cinema, possibly a boat trip. Tom and Lauren would like a day's boat trip. We could take the one that crosses the *étang* to catch market day in Sète or an early morning fishing trip if that's what they fancy.

"Maman," that familiar little voice shouts from behind me. Josette rushes past and into arrivals where a heavily pregnant woman is waiting by the door.

"Chérie," Josette's father calls out in French with a Yorkshire accent. "You shouldn't be driving. I said we'd take the tram."

He holds her face and kisses her. Then he strokes her belly and kisses her again.

"Josette," she says. "What have you done with your hair? It's a mess."

"No, it isn't," Josette replies. "This is shabby chic. It's how they do it in Leeds. Oh, Maman, you're so old-fashioned."

Their happiness is like a gift from the gods. I watch them walk away and I am filled with warmth. I know that, somewhere in Yorkshire, the grandmother who was waiting for Josette's arrival is looking forward to meeting her new grandchild for the first time. Like me, she is smiling.

Christmas Haunt

*At Christmas play and make good cheer, for Christmas
comes but once a year*
Thomas Tusser 1525-1580

Always at the corner of my eye. A blurred thing. A transitory image of something vague but when I turn my head to look at it, there's nothing there. Try as I might I can find nothing. Something rushes past me but I can never see what it is.

I ignored it at first. *Just a trick of the light*, I told myself. Nothing to worry about. But it keeps happening. It's been three weeks now. This ephemeral thing at the corner of my eye. Like a mirage. It moves so fast I can never get a good look at it. Every night it comes. Every *night*. Never during the day.

Christmas is near and all the television channels are full of the same stuff as every year. I haven't bothered with a tree or fairy lights. Can't be bothered with all that rigmarole. Decorations? There'd only be me to look at them. So I look at the box instead. Every night I sit with my coffee and watch the Christmas specials. I've seen them all before. Even the newest ones seem old, somehow. They play just like all the other repeats. Year after year they roll out the same old same old. And just as I'm feeling like I'm also part of the rerun, the blurred mirage flickers just at the edge of my sight.

I try a rational approach.

Oh, you're just tired. You've spent too long watching the box and now your eyes are going funny. That's all it is. Maybe you need new glasses.

But there it goes again at the corner of my eye and this time I think,

Next time, don't move your head to look at it. It can see you moving. Keep still. Just move your eyes.

And so, on the sofa I sit sideways on to the television. I have to watch out sideways but my head is facing forwards so in my peripheral vision I'll be able to see whatever it is that keeps flashing around the edges of the room.

It's uncomfortable sitting like this but soon I get used to watching television out of one corner of my eye while I'm waiting for the blurred thing to happen. And I'm not going to let it catch me out again. This time I'll be ready and catch it and then I can put an end to all this wondering.

My neck is aching. It's sharp like toothache. I want to move but I know what will happen if I do.

It knows.

It knows I want to move and as soon as I do . . .

My shoulders are aching now as well as my neck and there's a pain running down my right side. My muscles are tensing. I might get cramp. If I budge just a little, I'll feel more relaxed. I lean back on the sofa and THERE IT GOES.

At the corner of my eye a blurred, shimmering thing races around the skirting and disappears before I can get a good look at it.

It was waiting, I think.

It had to be waiting for me to make that move because as soon as I shifted my position on the sofa it knew it could come out and do that blurred, shimmery thing as it raced past me. I make myself another hot drink and I sit in my kitchen to think about the shape of the thing.

Shifting.

Its shape shifts.

Yes. It's a silent shape shifter that won't let you see it. It won't be pinned down.

Stubborn. A bit like me, I think. Suddenly I know what it is and make myself laugh aloud at the impertinence of it. The answer forms itself in my mind as if it wasn't me who'd thought it. Why hadn't I thought of that before? It all seems so clear to me now. So now I know what it is I suppose it'll stop its nightly flight around my sitting room once I've done what it wants me to do.

It isn't easy climbing the loft ladder without help. I remember the times when we'd wait till long after the kids were asleep and Steve would hold the ladder steady while I scrambled up. He was too big to get through the hatch so that bit was always my job. I'd pass everything down to him and then we'd have a nice drink together while we finished off the wrapping and put out the piles under the tree. I know there's a smile on my face now as I recall those Christmases past. I can smile at them now. Those days are long gone but, at least, I still have the memories. I'll always have those. Wouldn't it be sadder still not to have even the memories?

The blurred, shimmering thing is up there in the loft. I know it is. I can't see it yet but I know that's where it goes whenever I try to look at it. I know it does. It's waiting for me and I'm still laughing and it doesn't matter that there's only me to see because I feel better already. Carefully, I retrace my steps with the box in my arms. Steve isn't behind me to help me with it so I have to manoeuvre the thing so it slides down the loft ladder a bit at a time while I prop it up. Then I let it slide down the carpet to the living room. I open the box and take out the pieces. Sort them into size. Short branches for the top, bigger ones below.

There's a bulb blinking near the top. I'll find a replacement tomorrow. In my living room I stand back to admire my handiwork.

"Grandma," a little voice says, "you've put up your tree!"

"I didn't hear you come in," I say. "Is your mother here?"

"She's just coming."

I hurry for a tissue. Steve is in my eyes and all I can see is blurred and shimmery.

Resolution

Many people look forward to the new year for a new start on old habits.
Author unknown

He screwed up his eyes at me as if I had no sense at all.
"Why do I need to make a resolution?" he said.
"It's like a promise to yourself, Andy."
"I know what it is. I asked why you think *I* need to make one. Making promises to oneself hardly seems sensible."
"Some people want to lose weight, for instance, or learn a new skill. Things like that. Making a resolution makes it more formal."
"They can do that at any time."
"Well, it's what everybody does at this time of year," I said. "You know, a new year, a new start."
I tried to sound hopeful but I saw his face crease and his mouth turned in on itself the way it does when he's getting *literal*.
"Everybody? You can't possibly know that."
"It's just a figure of speech, darling," I said. "Look, never mind."
I attempted to move away, to switch on TV or something but he wasn't having any of that.
"Only people who are having problems should make resolutions," he said, his voice growing louder.
I know better than to ask him to explain his thinking. There's no need. He's going to spell it out anyway, whether I wish it or no.
"A resolution," he said, "is a RE- solution. In other words, the solution you had before is no longer working and you have to find a new one."
Once we've reached this stage there's no point arguing with him. My stomach was churning. I put on the kettle for a calming cup of peppermint tea.

"People don't use language properly," he was saying, but I'd stopped listening. I didn't hear the rest of his exposition although I could guess where it was going.

I took my tea into the living room but he followed me, still spouting his beliefs as if they were the only opinions that mattered. When he'd finished I gave him my sweetest smile.

"Thank you, Andy," I said. "I'm glad we've cleared that up."

"Cleared what up?" he said.

"Our difference of opinion about resolutions."

"There was nothing to clear," he said. "I've always known where I stand on this matter."

When he walked off he did that funny little skip he does when he's feeling pleased with himself. He raises up onto his toes and sets off with a pronounced hop, at the same time ducking his head and bobbing like a pigeon. It's a dead giveaway and he must know it makes him look odd but he's done it since he was three and now he's twelve it's as much a part of him as the colour of his eyes.

I sigh and finish my tea.

I am resolved not to cry.

PROMISES, PROMISES

He that promises most will perform least
Gaelic proverb

You promised me undying love
as you looked into my eyes.
I didn't know that beer could talk
and that it was brewer's lies.

You promised me a flash new car,
a Beamer or a Jag,
but you'd been on the pop again
and it was brewer's brag.

You promised me a holiday
to Disney for a week,
but it all got pissed against the wall
because of brewer's leak.

You promised me a diamond ring,
but it's made of coloured glass,
'cos yer mates mean more than I do.
You're a first rate brewer's ass.

You promised me we'd buy a home,
a pretty, smart new house,
but the cash went straight across the bar.
You're a lying, brewer's louse.

You promised me a Wedding Day
with a great big family feast.
You might as well have farted,
You're so stuffed with brewer's yeast.

You promised me an orgasm.
Now, ladies, am I right?
Brewer's droop don't hit the spot.
Some blokes are fulla shite!

A Gentle Message

A mother's hug lasts long after she lets go.
Author unknown

My mother was the first child born to Florence and Michael O'Driscoll. They'd already chosen a name for her but a visiting nurse said the baby's eyes reminded her of when she was a child on her father's farm and had a pet calf with large, soft eyes like that. So my mother was nicknamed Molly and that's how she was known from that day on. I must have been about ten years old before I learned Molly wasn't her real name. I once asked her whether or not she minded being named after a heifer and she said,

"I've grown into *Molly,* don't you think? Anyway, nobody knows my real name. They wouldn't know who you were talking about. What's the point in changing now?"

Molly inherited the O'Driscoll love of travel. *News-bearers* is the old meaning for the Irish name Ó hEidersceoil. In those days they must have had to travel on horseback or on foot to spread the news but Molly loved to travel just to find out what was there. From her early years she saved every penny in order to discover what was beyond that range of hills and what the town at the end of the train line looked like. She loved music, too and by the time I was old enough to travel with her we'd be off to see touring companies, especially when they might feature any of the performers who lodged with us when I was a girl. I have such happy memories of my childhood. Our house was always full of travel plans, music and Molly's friends.

I never knew my Irish grandfather. He died when I was still a baby but I inherited the O'Driscoll preferences, too. I grew to love opera and musical theatre. As for travel, to me, the journey is more exciting than the arrival. Like my mother, I love going to places just to see what's there. If that journey coincides with a music festival I'm in seventh heaven. It's strange how these preferences pass on through the generations but I don't believe scientists have yet discovered how it happens. We know there's a gene for blue eyes, for example, but is there one for the love of toe-tapping music?

When I was eleven Mum and I boarded a coach from West Yorkshire to London to go to the Palladium Theatre where my favourite pop star was performing. Mum queued with me afterwards at the stage door waiting for autographs and I remember that was the first time I'd ever felt gawky and embarrassed about wearing short, white ankle socks when all the other fans were proper teenagers who had on stiletto heels as high as their backcombed hair. There was a large crowd of them, all boisterous and excited at seeing their idol close up, face to face. I remember how Mum shielded me from their pushing and shoving to get past us to the front of the queue. She threw her arms around me and shouted at the other fans to behave themselves. I still miss those strong, protective arms. When she died she left a huge emptiness in my life.

Forty years after that trip to London I'm sitting with a friend on another coach travelling to see a matinée musical show at The Palladium. My love of music has travelled with me through the years. I've seen all the West End shows. This revival of an old favourite is a must-see. If they needed an understudy I could probably march right up onto the stage and take over.

It's a beautiful spring day. Everything looks fresh and green and May sunshine feels warm on the coach window. There's all the anticipation of summer in the air and I'm feeling happy and excited. I'm looking forward to hearing some of my favourite musical theatre songs.

"Have you been to The Palladium before?" my friend Jan asks.

"Not for donkey's years," I say. I tell her about queuing for autographs when I was eleven. We reminisce a little about teenage years, pop stars of the time, the fashions we wore and the way we did our hair. We talk about Saturday jobs and first loves and I turn to look outside, my head full of images of that first visit, squashed in the queue at the stage door, my mother protecting me from those bigger, rowdier girls.

I wish you were still here, Mum.

I'm shocked at the thought. The words have shaped themselves in my mind. It's as if *I* haven't thought them. The sentiment simply arrives fully formed and I've had no say in it.

And the rest just follows.

So, show me where you've travelled to now, Mum. What's it like at the end of the line? Is everything all right? Let me know. Send me a message. Today.

I'm sitting there, staring out the coach window, having a one-sided conversation with a ghost as the M1 rumbles past beneath me but I am passionately serious. I really mean it. I want a message from my mother who's been dead for more than ten years. But I'm uncomfortable, too. To be honest, my solemnity is making me feel edgy. I've never done anything like this before. Never voiced my feelings about needing a message from beyond. I've always been sceptical about those things. But my thoughts are rushing on ahead of me.

Nothing too weird, Mum, I'm telling her. *You know I'll freak out if I see anything spooky. I'd like your message to be something more gentle, but something so obviously personal to us that it couldn't possibly be a coincidence.*

My friend, Jan brings out the chocolate eclairs and taps me on the shoulder. I stop staring outside and take one. After the rattling of sweetie papers and exaggerated sighs of chocolatey pleasure, there's a conversation about favourite musical shows but my thoughts keep slipping back to memories of my mother.

The first thing Jan wants to do when we arrive in London is go into Liberty's and treat herself. I've never been inside the store.

"Oh, you'll love it," Jan tells me and I follow on after her as she leads the way through the entrance and into the cosmetics department on the ground floor. The aroma is deliciously powdery. Very *girly*. Jan leads on through another doorway. I follow, catching her excitement at all the goodies on display.

My jaw drops. There's a *whole room* dedicated to lipsticks. I've never seen so many. There are brand names I've never heard of. A fashionable throng of women are inspecting testers and trying them out.

"You *must* be able to find something you want in here," Jan says.

"Well, I suppose I could do with a new summer lipstick," I agree.

Jan has a store shopping basket in her hand and is already dropping glossy packages into it. I make my way through the crowds over to the far wall and begin my search.

A nice, browny-pink for summer, I'm thinking. Nothing too loud. I play around with some testers but nothing hits the spot. I can't find a texture I like. Some are too dry with a matte finish. It might be the fashion to have lips that look as if they've been painted with emulsion but it's not for me. I can't find the colour I want either. I move to another display and repeat the process. No luck. I move on again.

In this whole room full of lipsticks are you telling me there's not one browny-pink?

There's a display of lipsticks by another company whose name is unfamiliar to me but I like the gun metal colour of the packaging. I try one on my hand.

This is the one.

I can only just make out the product number. My reading glasses are at the bottom of my bag and I try scrabbling for them. I've brought my big bag and I've been meaning to give it a sort out but it's full of stuff all in a muddle and my glasses have done a disappearing act. I can't find them. Instead I screw up my eyes and look on the shelf above the testers to find the matching number. I find the right one and take it to the cash desk to pay. Jan is still shopping. She's over the other side looking at lip gloss. I'm feeling pleased with my small purchase. Lipstick from Liberty's. Very swish.

I might as well put some on.

The chocolate eclairs have put paid to the lipstick I started out with. Now I really need my glasses to see what I'm doing.

My mother didn't need to look in a mirror to put on her lipstick, I recall.

I know where my mouth is, she'd say and I'd watch as she drew on a perfect outline - top lip first, bottom lip afterwards. Then she'd press her lips together and come up looking like Hollywood. Try as I might, I never learned how to do it. I need a mirror and here in Liberty's I need my glasses too. Miraculously, they're the first things my fingers find, tucked in a corner of my bag almost hidden in the lining.

I slide the package from its paper bag. I take out the lipstick from its little box and turn it over to read the label on the bottom to see what the colour is called.

The back of my neck goes cold. There's a shivering feeling running through my hair. My knees want to buckle. I put out my arm to steady myself against the cash counter. The room is spinning. My mouth has gone dry.

"Is everything all right, Madam?" a voice says. "Are you feeling ill?"

I can't answer. I lean against the cash counter to stop myself from falling. There's a small commotion around me. People are jostling. Their shapes are blurred and their voices are like white noise, not making any sense. Jan appears and takes my arm.

"Come on," she says. "Hold on to me."

I'm in a daze. It's an effort to walk in a straight line. We go outside into the fresh air.

"You've gone ever so pale," Jan says.

There's an Italian restaurant on Great Marlborough street and we go inside. I sink into a booth. My legs are still wobbly. We order strong coffee and a bottle of water. The water tastes sweet and cool. Jan hands me a tissue and I blow my nose. She waits a moment.

"Are you feeling better now?" Jan asks. "Your colour's coming back a bit."

"Thank you, yes."

I stir some sugar into my coffee and take a sip.

"What happened? Did you go faint? Is everything all right?"

"I've had a bit of a shock," I say. My heart has stopped hammering so fast now and I can breathe properly. I tell Jan what I was thinking during the coach journey.

"You got a message from your mother?" she says. "How?"

I delve into my handbag and bring out the lipstick.

"She led you to a lipstick? I don't understand."

I show Jan the label on the bottom. She reads it but looks puzzled.

Something must have got into my eyes inside the shop. Now I can see that the shade of lipstick I've just paid for isn't anywhere near a colour I would normally choose. Instead of the browny-pink I'd set out to find I've bought a blue lilac colour, one which doesn't suit me at all.

'I don't get it,' Jan says. 'The colour is called Iris.'

Iris.

My eyes are welling. I can feel my mouth stretch into a lopsided grin. This lipstick is the message I asked for. It is no coincidence. Iris is my mother's real name. The one nobody else knows. It's the gentlest message Molly could lead me to. Soft and warm as a kiss.

Over the Hill

Do not regret growing older. It is a privilege denied to many.
Author unknown

Mick put the final polish on his driver's cab and stood back to admire his handiwork. His face glowed with the effort of all that rubbing. Gleaming in spring sunshine the red and gold livery winked back at him. The brass bell on top shone golden and bright. Behind his cab all the passenger carriages lined up in smart precision by the kerb outside the lockup where he parked.

"You beauty," he said aloud and, after easing out the tightness of his shirt collar and loosening his tie, he put away his polishing cloth in a tool box under the seat in the front carriage. He reached for his jacket and stood for a moment to catch his breath and stretch his back.

'MICK'S TOURIST TRAIN' it said on the doors along each side. *'SEE THE VIEWS OVER THE BAY'.*

He adjusted his railway driver's style cap and fastened his jacket. It was a little snug. More than a little snug. He sighed and unfastened it again. He'd have to ask Kath to move the buttons again. His collars were tight, too. He was getting to look more like *the fat controller* with every passing year.

Old age creeping up, he thought. *Creeping up too fast.* He jutted out his chin and traced a circle with his neck to loosen the knots in his shoulders. Each morning it was getting worse and it took him longer to release the stiffness in his back. In cold weather it was even worse. But it was the first day of a new season and he didn't want to think about getting older. He had a lot more years left in him yet. Driving the road-train wasn't a taxing job. In fact, it was very pleasant on a beautiful day like today with a cobalt sky and only tiny puff-ball clouds scudding in the breeze. He shrugged away his fears. His little summer business bought with his redundancy money had provided him and Kath with that bit extra to see them through and he didn't see why he should have to think about the time when he wouldn't be able to do it. Surely those days were a long way away yet.

He climbed in and set off for the departure point on the promenade. People waved. They always waved at the road-train and he would ring the bell and wave back. Sometimes, he'd see them hurrying away and he knew they'd be at the departure point before him, waiting to get on for the ride.

The return journey lasted just over an hour and a half depending on traffic. On the way up, as the road train climbed steadily up the hill overlooking the pretty fishing village, he'd slow further to allow for photographs. He'd point out landmarks as they trundled slowly upwards and remark on fabulous architect designed houses behind their elaborate gates. His travellers would murmur their pleasure at having seen first hand the house where a famous person was born. Celebrities were few and far between these days but there was still a famous musician and an author in permanent residence in the resort. Generally though, the holiday trade had shifted. People wanted other things nowadays and when he saw on television how some holiday destinations on pretty islands abroad had turned into all-night partying sessions, he was glad the old place didn't get that sort of tourist.

First run of the day was at ten-thirty am. There was a small queue waiting at the departure kiosk. He pulled over and stopped.

"Hop on," he called to the young couple and family of four. "I've got a booking for thirty this morning at one of the hotels but there are enough seats for everybody. I'll be along to give you your tickets in a minute."

The little girl with her big brother and parents made an excited bee-line to the front. Children loved the road train. He often thought that if you took small children in the family car to look at smart houses and the view of the bay from the top of the hill, they wouldn't be the least interested. But sit them in an open-sided carriage that rumbled over cobbles and squeezed through narrow streets, that was entirely different. Couples liked the trip, too. Younger twosomes would cuddle up close and be romantic. Older couples would enjoy taking the weight off tired legs. If you hadn't had to make the climb on foot, the view was even more magnificent when you still had breath to appreciate it.

He reached for his money pouch and took fares. The family of four were in the first carriage right behind his cab. The little girl smiled up at him but the boy had his head buried in a portable gaming machine. The young couple had gone all the way to the back. Mick smiled and remembered the days when he and Kath would always do that on coach trips or when they went to the cinema. Kath was manageress at the café on the peak overlooking the bay. She'd have some coffee waiting for him when he arrived with his first load of passengers.

"All aboard," he shouted. "Keep your hands and your head inside the carriage at all times."

He pulled away from the kerb and made off toward Hotel Belvedere. He rang the bell and a group of teenagers waved. He rang the bell again.

"Wait!" a voice shouted behind him. "Driver, please stop."

He pulled in at the nearest convenient place along the sea front. The little girl in the front carriage was in tears.

"I'm so sorry," her father explained. "My daughter has dropped her teddy. Back at the kiosk, we think. Can you give me a minute and I'll run back for him? Ted goes everywhere with us."

"Well, I don't know," Mick said.

"We keep a photograph album of all the places Ted's been. You know, Ted at the beach, Ted at the cinema, the funfair. Last year he went to the top of Blackpool tower. My daughter's afraid he'll get run over if we leave him. Please just give me a minute to fetch him."

Mick looked at his watch. The party at the hotel would be waiting. He had to keep to his schedule or it threw out the rest of the day.

"Well," he said, "I shouldn't really."

But the child's sobs were so endearing. "All right," he said. "Quick as you can."

Minutes ticked by. There was no sign of the child's father. Mick looked at his watch again. Ten minutes now. He could hear the girl's mother doing her best to pacify her daughter. He climbed down from his cab and looked back along the promenade as if the act of looking could make the father return sooner. Nearly fifteen minutes now. Eventually he returned, panting.

"I do apologise," he said. "Somebody had picked up Ted already. They were going to hand him in. I had the devil of a job to convince them Ted belongs to us."

The child reached out for her toy and held him close.

"Thank you, Daddy,' she said. "And thank you, Mister for waiting for my daddy."

The joy in her eyes was a picture. Mick felt suddenly proud. A few minutes delay was nothing compared with that little girl's happy face.

"What's your name, sweetheart?" Mick said.

"Emma."

"Well, you hold on to Ted good and tight now, Emma. Do you hear? We don't want him falling out when we go uphill. He'd roll all the way back down to the bottom and then what would we do?"

He glanced at the young couple in the rear carriage. They were watching intently and smiling at one another. He grasped the situation straight away. There was no baby bump visible but Mick knew by the light in their eyes they were expecting their first.

Sometimes, it felt so good to be alive, to be part of the story of humanity, to witness it happening all around him. He climbed in his cab and pulled out into the road feeling contented with his lot and with life in general. On a day like today it wouldn't be right to start worrying again about growing older.

He turned the corner by the bakery and rolled along the avenue behind the promenade. He passed the bicycle hire shop and the row of souvenir shops, on past the arcades and tea shops, pizza palaces and fish and chips, bars and night clubs, pubs and restaurants. Pavements were filling up. People were making the most of this lovely weekend weather. In an hour or so the air would fill with the mixed aromas of cooking: the savoury tang of frying onions and powdery sweet candy floss at the fast food outlets; the mouth-watering smell of roast dinners from the restaurants.

At the traffic lights he turned back onto the promenade and into the drive at Hotel Belvedere.

He could hear the group of thirty before he could see them. As he followed the crescent he saw them, scattered either side of the curving drive, spilling onto the flower beds. A woman in a track suit and carrying a stick with a fluffy pom-pom on top was trying to gather them all together. Mick slowed as he approached the building.

"Can you get everybody over to the right-hand side, please?" he called to the woman. She didn't hear him over the clamour of twenty nine excited voices. "Wait on that side, please," he repeated and pointed.

"I want to get on at *this* side, Mrs Sullivan. I always like to sit at *this* side," a voice whined.

"Harry," the woman in charge said, "the driver wants us to wait on the other side."

"I'm staying here. I always like to sit at *this* side," Harry said and folded his arms across his chest.

Harry's friends must have thought the same because they wouldn't budge, either. Others began running across to join Harry's group, confusing their left from their right, it seemed.

Mick climbed down and approached the woman.

"Hello," she said. "I'm Mary. We're all in a bit of a muddle I'm afraid."

"I need everybody over there," Mick said and pointed again. "It's a tight corner getting back out into the road. I have to keep sharp left."

Mary didn't have much authority over her group, Mick thought. They were still ignoring his request.

"Why won't Harry do as he's told?" Mick heard Emma ask her mother.

"I don't know, darling. Perhaps he doesn't quite understand."

"We can't go anywhere until you all move over to *that* side," Mick shouted. "I have to get this long train safely round the bend."

That did the trick. Some of Harry's friends pulled him across to the other side of the drive, Harry grumbling all the way. Mick manoeuvred the carriages tight up close to the building.

They fought for positions. Argued over which carriage. Who wanted to sit with whom. Who didn't want to sit next to whom.

"I need the toilet," one of them said and shot off into the hotel reception. When he re-emerged Mick's road-train passengers were all finally settled. Mary was looking exhausted as she stood waiting while Mick checked that all the chains across the carriages were properly secured.

"Couldn't you have rung the hotel to let us know you were going to be late?" she asked.

"I didn't think that would be necessary," he said.

"They get so agitated, you see."

Mick *could* see.

"It's a big responsibility, being in charge of such a large group," Mick said.

"Oh, I'm not on my own. Candy helps me."

She put her arm around the slight figure standing next to her. Candy beamed.

"I'm Mrs Sullivan's helper," she said. "I look after everybody's spending money. I'm good with numbers and, anyway, they forget."

Her voice was as thin as her limbs. Mick wondered how Candy coped with someone like rumbustious Harry.

The journey uphill passed without further interruption. Mick heard the usual 'oohs' and 'aahs' as they passed the imposing gates of Lark Hall and through the speaker system he told them who it was that lived there. He stopped and while they were taking photographs of the gate he pulled out his mobile and called Kath.

"There are thirty of them," he told her.

She said they were prepared at the café. They'd made up extra sandwiches and had a full supply of hot drinks at the ready.

"They're a bit, erm, difficult to deal with." Mick kept his voice to a whisper.

Kath wanted to know what Mick meant. He didn't know how to say it without offending someone if they overheard his response.

"Somewhat over-excitable, I'd say."

"We'll manage," Kath said. "Don't worry."

He put away his phone and moved off. The road climbed like a snake with sharp hairpin bends. As they climbed higher the breeze freshened.

"Nearly at the top, folks," he said over the speaker system. "There'll be a short break for snacks and a drink. Toilets are inside the café. Please remain seated until I come to a complete stop and remove the chains."

He negotiated the final steep climb and tight bend at the top. The breeze was always even stiffer up here. He definitely needed those jacket buttons moving or else wear a warm fleece instead. He pulled in at his usual parking place and walked along the length of the train, unfastening the carriage chains.

"Fifteen minutes, everybody," he called out and hung back till all his passengers had made their move. He watched Candy leading the way, purse in hand. Mary brought up the rear with her pom-pom stick. Harry was at the front of the crocodile, his voice louder than all the others put together.

Kath was waiting inside with his coffee. He took a seat by the window while Kath and her assistant dealt with their customers. At the table next to him Emma waited with her brother while their parents were being served. Emma had propped up Ted so he could see out of the window. Her brother was still tapping at his computer game. At the counter the rowdy group of thirty were arguing over sandwiches and cakes and where they were going to sit.

"Why do they do that?" Mick heard Emma ask her brother.

155

"Do what?" the boy said without looking up from his game.

"Behave like little children."

"That's what happens when you get old."

"No, it doesn't."

"Sometimes it does."

Their parents arrived with trays of snacks and drinks. Emma's brother focussed back on his game.

"Mummy," Emma said, "You know the man called Harry and all the others? Why are they like little children? Oliver says that's what happens when you get old but I know it isn't because granddad isn't like that."

Mick waited for the ensuing silence to end. He made a point of drinking his coffee and looking the other way. He didn't know how he would have answered Emma's question, either. Emma's mother did a little cough.

"Well," she said, "it isn't anything for you to worry about, darling. But, it does happen sometimes to some people."

"And do they know it's happening?"

Ah, the joy of innocence, Mick thought.

The answer was a long time coming.

"I don't know the answer to that, sweetheart. Would you like me to find out for you when we get home? I don't want you to worry about it."

"I'm not worried, Mummy. I think it's nice."

"Nice?"

Mick gulped. He recognised the depth of surprise in Emma's mother's voice. He couldn't imagine what the child was going to come out with next.

"Well," she began, "when you're a child other people look after you, don't they? So if you get to be a child again when you're an old person, other people will look after you again."

Another long silence followed. Across the other side of the café the group were taking noisy turns in going to the toilet. Some went outside to take more photographs and there was much chattering and laughter and scraping of chairs.

"And," Emma added as she watched them, "you get to play out again."

Out of the mouth of babes.
Kath came to join him.

"Everything all right?" she asked him and picked up his empty cup. "Have you time for a fill-up before you go?"

He put his arm around her shoulder.

"Everything's just perfect," he said. "I'll have a bacon sandwich on my next trip if you've time. And will you move these jacket buttons for me when you get a minute?"

"I'll do it tonight," she said.

"Well," Mick said, "On second thoughts. . . There's no rush, Kath. In fact, I can wear something else. Forget I said it."

"But you always like to wear that jacket."

I always like to sit at this side.

The words were like an echo in Mick's head.

"Well then," he said, "maybe it's time to be more flexible. It's not the end of the world if I wear something else to work. Is it?"

"Just as you like, love," she said. "Two rashers or three when you come back?"

"Two. And an egg, please."

Mick helped Mary Sullivan gather up her flock and get them safely seated in their carriages. He fastened the chains and had a kind word with all his happy passengers as he walked along the length of *Mick's Tourist Train*. When he reached the front he stopped.

"Excuse me," he said to the family of four and Emma in particular. "Do you think Ted might like to help me drive? I can't invite people to sit in my cab with me. That's against the rules. But there's no rule about Teds. You could take a picture for his photograph album."

"That would be lovely," Emma's mother said.

Mick took off his tie and wrapped it around Emma's teddy bear. He adjusted the fabric so that the *driver* badge showed clearly on Ted's chest.

"Thank you. You must give me your email address so we can send you the photo."

"I'd like that very much. Yes. Very much indeed."

The rest of the road train journey was all downhill.

Just like my own, Mick thought as he moved off and made for the first tight hairpin bend. But from now on he was going to make sure he enjoyed the ride. Why waste precious time worrying?

Blank Canvas

Silence is the mother of truth
Benjamin Disraeli 1804-1881

I don't like keeping secrets. And I don't like lies. Why should anybody who's always tried to live a good life and never intentionally done anything to hurt another person have something to hide? I've always thought honesty is the best policy when dealing with other people's opinions, others' emotions. With tact, it goes without saying. Sometimes you have to be diplomatic. I don't like being blunt.

But right now, right here, I *am* going to be blunt.

I'm keeping a secret. After all these years and all I've just said, I'm not being totally honest. But there's a very good reason for that.

I didn't plan to be divorced in my forties. It wasn't what I wanted. I'd already been through the mill, as they say. My first husband died and left me a childless widow when I was in my early thirties. I know such tragedies happen to many others and we all have to learn to move on but if it hadn't been for my best friend, Maria, I would have struggled to cope.

"I know you don't feel like going out, Bridget," she'd say to me , "but you need some fresh air."

And I'd let her make me put on my coat. She'd thrust a hairbrush into my hand and I'd pull it through my tangle of hair. Then she'd bundle me into the passenger seat of her car and off we'd go. We usually finished up somewhere with a tearoom, often a garden centre where Maria would always find some specimen plant she had the ideal place for. Her garden grew and matured just as our friendship and, I have to admit, learning about her plants and how to take care of them helped me regain my own strength after my bereavement. I took up my work again, illustrating books for children. Often my designs featured shrubs and flowers I'd only recently learned about.

I always thought Maria and her husband Dan were solid. They'd had their daughter, Ruth when they were both very young. I suppose my crisis in my thirties helped Maria through her own empty nest grief when Ruth went off to university abroad. In a way, I guess I was Ruth's replacement. Maria needed someone to look after and I filled the gap in her life. I used to feel a bit envious of Maria and Dan's comfortable relationship. They were so at ease with one another. Then, one day in autumn he went out to buy firelighters, he said, and never came back. Maria and I found out through social media he was living with another woman. Some friend of a friend had posted photographs of their housewarming party and there they were, Dan and this new woman, happy and smiling for all the world to see.

Maria was devastated. Our personal situations suddenly reversed. Now it was my turn to be comforter.

"Do you think it was a good idea to print out those pictures?" I said to her one grim afternoon when she was gazing at the photos again, her eyes brimming with tears.

"I can't help it," she said. "Just look at them. All his family were there with him and . . . *her*. His sister and brother-in-law. His nephews. His brothers. They must have all known what was going on. I feel betrayed by each and every one of them."

It's easy to say things like *you're better off without them* but such platitudes don't help lessen the pain.

"I don't know what to say," I said instead, "other than I would feel exactly the same as you do. The pain feels unbearable, I know. But you will bear it. You have to. There's no escaping the suffering. You have to feel it. You have to let it happen. It's the only way to get through it and come out the other side with your sanity intact."

I remember she slumped over on her sofa. Her shoulders heaved with the weight of her pain. I took the printouts from her. Later I would destroy them and persuade her to unfriend all the people in the photographs so she couldn't be upset by further images of her husband enjoying his happy new life. I also remember thinking how callous it was of him to treat Maria that way. I didn't understand the ease with which he had so utterly discarded her. The man must have no compassion to be able to move on so rapidly as though his years with Maria meant nothing.

In time we resumed our trips to the garden centre tearooms. The first spring outing after Dan had left stands out in my mind. We began the day in high spirits. The sun was doing its best, the fresh, bright green of burgeoning springtime clothing trees and shrubs along the lanes as if nature were telling us to be happy. Maria had received good news from her daughter and a happy photograph of Ruth on a field trip with a motley crew of student types covered in mud in a group selfie all grinning at the camera. They were investigating the ecological impact of two years' regulations regarding the clearing of a silted-up river bed. Our conversation during the short car journey led to water plants and how Maria had always wanted to have some kind of water feature in her garden. I felt she'd made a giant stride forward and I was delighted she seemed to be moving through her grief and onwards out of her sadness. She parked her car and we decided to have coffee before we browsed the bedding plant section. We took the short cut past the trolleys and piles of grow-bags.

Maria stopped in her tracks. Her back went rigid as she stood, staring at heaps of compost bags. The rest happened in slow-motion as her body went limp. She looked as if she was crumpling before my eyes. She almost fell to her knees. I thought she was going to faint. She doubled over, clutched at her stomach and dashed away into the car park where I found her in floods of tears.

"What's happened?" I said.

She struggled to speak.

"Sorry. It was the potting compost. Dan always used to help me lift the heavy bags."

"Well, you've got me now," I said. "If you want to buy compost we will. And we'll manage between us."

It's strange how sometimes it's the little inconsequential things which bring back the strongest memories to remind you of your pain. We found the muscle to lift the huge bags of compost that day and the bond between us deepened further. She was like my big sister. A sort of sister-mum. We had come to rely on one another for support in so many ways.

Maria went from strength to strength. She regained her positive outlook, sorted her finances after the decree absolute and bought a pretty new-build on the outskirts of town not far from our favourite garden centre where their crumbly soft home-made scones and Bakewell tart were an absolute joy. Dan was now the ex. That's what she called him. Never by name; just *the ex*. She stopped talking about him altogether eventually. Her mind was full of her new home and what she was planning indoors and out. She relished the blank canvas of her empty plot.

Then I met Callum.

I've read about women saying they were 'swept off their feet' and never quite understood what that meant. With my first marriage our feelings grew steadily towards being a couple planning our lives together. I'd never experienced a heady rush of overpowering emotions. That's not to say I didn't love him but it was a quiet kind of love. A natural progression.

Callum came into my life like an explosion. Very quickly we felt so right for one another. He listened so attentively to everything I said and, if I'd had such a thing as an ideal man checklist, he'd have ticked every box. I could hardly believe such a wonderful man had dropped into my life as if it was meant to be. So, when I tried explaining to Sally how quickly I felt very attached to him it was difficult to find the right words.

"But you hardly know him," she said to me. "How can you be thinking about living together?"

"I've never met anyone like him," was all I could say.

"Please be careful," she said. "Please promise me you'll be careful."

Right from the beginning of our relationship Callum made me feel so special. In a matter of a few short weeks he was talking in terms of *we* rather than *I*. After three months he moved in with me and we began to plan our wedding. Each evening when he came home from his work in the city we'd plan our future together.

I must have been hungry for love but just didn't realise it. I suppose that made me vulnerable. I believed Callum when he told me how much he loved me and wanted nothing more than for me to be his wife. We planned to open a joint account and I understood that his commitment to provide for his former wife and two children meant he wouldn't be able to pay in as much as me. We were to be man and wife and would share everything. Why would I think there was anything wrong with that?

Six months after we met we announced our engagement and set the date to be married on my fortieth birthday a few months later. Neither of us thought there was any sense in waiting longer. We wanted to grab the opportunity life had thrown our way and make the most of it. We were so in love. Life was bliss. He showered me with love and attention. He'd surprise me with small gifts or a meal he'd cooked himself. He'd bring home a little something he'd seen in a shop window just because he knew I'd like it. We opened the joint account. And he changed.

He began to find fault. First he criticised Maria. He didn't like that she took up too much of my time.

"She's my dearest friend, Callum," I told him. "She's helped me through some very difficult times."

"Those times are over now," he said. "Why does she have to call you so much? You don't have to go over there every week either. Sometimes I think you care more about her and her garden than you do about me."

I tried to make him see that wasn't true. How could he not know how much I loved him?

Then he found fault with me. Whereas I'd been his perfect woman, the one he'd searched for all his life, now I wasn't attentive enough. I didn't keep house the way he expected. He was disappointed with my cleaning standards. I must be planning to abandon him because I had a separate, personal bank account. I wasn't putting everything into our relationship the way I'd promised him.

He withdrew from me. He withheld all tokens of affection. He wouldn't even touch me and shrank back from me whenever I tried to get close. Then, out of the blue, just as I was feeling desperate about how things had gone so wrong and wondering how that had happened, he'd put his arm around my shoulder, kiss me and tell me something nice. After weeks of being ignored those small gestures made me feel that everything was going to be all right after all. I settled for his crumbs of comfort.

I didn't talk to Maria about what was happening at home. I should have. Maybe she'd have been able to make me see sense. If I'd been thinking straight I'd have realised how foolish it was of me to close my personal banking account and, in an effort to show my husband he meant everything to me, put everything into our joint account.

The last day he and I had together comes back to me still in nightmares. I'd been out shopping with Maria. I was feeling great. I'd bought new underwear to please my husband. The night before, Callum had held me in his arms and told me he loved me. We kissed and made love the way it used to be in the beginning. My heart soared. I felt everything was going to be wonderful again. The cold March day darkly threatened snow and after I'd dropped Sally off at her house I was looking forward to getting home into the warmth and being with my husband.

My house was in darkness. I walked up the path wondering why Callum hadn't put on the lights. He'd said he was going to cook for us that night as he was finishing work early. I stepped into the kitchen into silent darkness. No cooking smells. No heating on. No radio or television sounds. Nothing. I reached for the light switch.

A hand grabbed my wrist. Out of the blackness his face loomed before me. I remember a shiver running down my back and feeling afraid.

"I've been waiting for you," he said. The threatening tone in his voice further alarmed me. I didn't know what he was going to do. Terror froze me.

"In the dark? Why? What are you doing?" I tried to speak calmly but my stomach was churning. Something was terribly wrong. My mouth dried and I could feel my legs beginning to shake.

He brought his face so close to mine that even through the gloom I could see the hideous desolation in his eyes, cold and empty, like dark hollows in his head.

"I'm leaving you." He grinned. A frightening, dreadful, victorious grimace.

I caught my breath. I didn't follow him outside as he left. I hardly dare move from the spot. I stood like a statue in the dark, silent kitchen. In my heart I knew it was finally over. In my head I knew I should be glad to be rid of him. He'd turned into a monster. I'd never forget what was behind the mask he'd cultivated to deceive me, that vicious look on his face, the dark gleam of triumph in those eyes. I switched on the light.

The house was empty. Callum had stripped it completely bare. I ran from room to room, gasping at the sight of my home ransacked, gutted of furniture, all my paintings torn from the wall, shattered glass on the floors. He'd even ripped out the phone. I sank onto the floor and sobbed.

I called Maria on my mobile. I was still on the floor when she arrived. I waited while she made her own tour of the house and I could hear her swearing as she moved around from room to room.

"Please don't say I told you so," I said when she came and sat on the floor beside me.

"I wouldn't dream of saying that," she said and put her arms round me. "You're coming home with me. Has he left you your clothes?"

They were in piles on the bedroom floor: he'd taken the wardrobes and drawers. We filled up some dustbin bags with enough of my clothes for a few days.

"Don't leave your car here," Maria said, "or he'll have that too, if he comes back. Do you think you'll be able to drive?"

I don't remember the drive to her house: I was on automatic pilot. When we got in she poured us two large shots and we sat in her living room talking until the early hours.

"In the morning we'll call the police," she said, "Although I don't hold out much hope."

"What do you mean?" I asked.

"I've been thinking. On the way over here, I've been wondering what he might do next. I don't think he will come back. He'll be long gone. You can't bring charges against someone unless you can find them. He's had this planned down to the last detail. You can bet on that."

"I suppose you're right. He's played me for a fool, hasn't he?"

"I'm afraid so, Bridget, my love. I think he probably had this planned right from the beginning."

My stomach lurched. I recalled all the times Callum had criticised me, rejected me, made me feel lacking. Maria was right. He had manipulated me all along. I thought about all the occasions I'd considered telling her how Callum was treating me and then deciding against. I should have told her. I should have swallowed my foolish pride and told my friend the truth instead of pretending everything was all right.

"Maria," I said. "I've transferred what was in my personal account to the joint account."

"He still has access to it of course?"

"Yes. He has a card."

She threw back her head and swore again.

"Bridget," she said, 'Get on my laptop right now this minute and check your account."

I hammered in my online banking details and password. The page opened. I could feel my jaw drop.

"It's empty, isn't it?" Maria said.

I nodded.

"I've been such a fool," I said.

"No. You haven't been a fool. You've been the victim of a heartless fraudster. We must go to your bank first thing and get the debit card stopped. If he puts it in a cash machine it'll get swallowed."

I hardly slept that night. I knew there'd be more trouble to come.

As well as emptying our joint account Callum had run it into overdraft. He'd made a lot of purchases including a one-way flight to Madrid for that very morning. I remember I looked at my watch. He'd be there, striding out into his new life after ruining mine.

The woman in the bank was as helpful as she could be but explained that as it was a joint account I'd be held responsible for repayment of the debts in Callum's absence. She put a stop on the card so it would be confiscated if he should try to get cash from an automatic dispenser and we could stop online transactions but we couldn't stop him from using it in stores to pay for goods. I lived on tenterhooks for months wondering what was going to happen next until, at last, the card reached its expiry date.

I stayed with Maria. I had to sell my home to pay back the bank for all the things Callum bought with the card on his travels around Europe and beyond. The police told me he must have had multiple passports and other fake documents. They'd come across stories like mine before where unsuspecting partners, male and female, had been taken in by criminals like Callum. It was usually impossible to trace their movements in time to have them apprehended. I discovered that throughout the time we were together he didn't have work in the city nor did he have an ex wife and two children to support. I had been duped. Callum, if that was his real name, was nothing more than a callously cold con-man. He was a predator, living at other people's expense, cheating and lying to get what he wanted and then moving swiftly on to his next victim.

Sun streams through the conservatory window where I sit painting a study of dragonflies for a children's book on the life cycle of insects. Maria's house is calm, peaceful after the recent visit from Ruth and her new boyfriend. We've had music and trips to the theatre, walks in the park, barbecues and real ale in the village pub. I've laughed till my sides ached and loved every minute of what has felt like honest-to-goodness family time.

Now, gentle breezes waft through the open patio doors and I can hear the tinkling splash of water from Maria's garden water feature and, further off, the thrum of a lawnmower. Maria is out there now putting stripes on her lawn, the original blank canvas of her plot now a thing of beauty, resplendent in its summer finery, magnificent with its contrasting shapes and colours under a leafy pattern of light and shade.

I clean my brush and mix a small amount of turquoise for highlights on my dragonfly's wings.

"Mummy! Mummy. I've seen one. It's there now. On the fountain."

"What is, darling?" I ask her.

"That thing. Like in your picture. You can see the colours in its wings. Come and look."

I rise from my seat and take hold of her hand and we go out together to look at the dragonfly by the fountain.

"Will it bite?" she asks.

"No, Tilly, it won't bite. But let's not get too close. We don't want to frighten it, do we?"

She stands with me, still holding onto my hand, gazing at the exotic creature in our garden and, finally, as the dragonfly flits away she claps her little hands as if nature had put on the show just for us.

"Is your picture finished yet?" she says.

"Nearly. Do you want to see it?"

She trots off to pass judgement on my painting. She stands with her weight on one leg, her arms folded and her head on one side, just the way I do when I'm assessing my work.

"So, what do you think, Tilly?"

"I think you're right. It isn't finished." And off she trots again outside.

My darling Tilly. She isn't finished yet, either. Four years old now and full of sparkling energy and curiosity. She is my daughter, my darling only child and I will do everything I can to see she grows into a happy, healthy young woman. She doesn't know who her father is. I told her he died and when I speak of him it's my first husband I'm remembering. For now, she accepts what I tell her. I know the day will come when she questions me about exactly when her father died and how it is that she could be born so long after his death. Heaven forgive me, I will continue to lie.

It hurts me to lie to her. Sometimes I think deceiving her is no better than the way her father deceived me. But then I grow strong again in my determination to protect her from the painful truth. Maria has said she'll help me. We have an explanation ready for when she's old enough to understand the intricacies of self- impregnation from the frozen spermatozoa of a partner now deceased.

Of course I still question myself. I've thought long and hard. There've been times when I couldn't sleep for worrying whether I'm doing the right thing. Once you start with a fabricated story the lie has a habit of growing. It goes on forever. It has to. Does Tilly have the right to know the truth? Should she know the kind of man her father really is? How would it benefit her to have that knowledge? How could a child be happy knowing what her father did to me? Wouldn't she worry that she might grow up to be just like him? I think knowing the truth would sour her joyful view of life, steal away her innocence. I'm convinced it's better to let her believe her father was a loving, caring man, one who would be so proud of her. One she can be proud of learning about.

It doesn't matter to me what anybody else thinks. You must make up your own mind about what you would do if you found yourself in my shoes. Tilly is *my* blank canvas; the most beautiful picture I have ever created. A work in progress. I marvel at her. When she smiles my world is full of beautiful light where there are no dark secrets and there is no need for lies.

Far be it from me

Everything that irritates us about others can lead us to an understanding of ourselves.
Carl Jung 1875-1961

Kevin had lost count how often he'd heard those five words. *Far be it from me*. They'd become part of every day life in the Mitchell household since Alison's mother had come to live with them.

"Far be it from me to criticise," she'd say, "but . . . "

And at that point Kevin would stop listening. Alison's mother, Shirley would be getting into her stride. He knew what would follow would be a lengthy diatribe full of the very thing Shirley insisted she didn't do. Criticise. She never stopped. It seemed to Kevin that Shirley spent her entire day criticising everything from television programmes they chose to watch to the food they ate.

He'd tried speaking to his wife about his concerns.

"It's bringing me down, love," he said one Saturday morning after Shirley had found fault with the way he was scrambling his eggs for breakfast. Alison wasn't there at that moment to hear her mother's latest complaint. She'd dashed out for Shirley's favourite bread which they'd forgotten to buy.

"I'm sorry, sweetheart," Alison said as she sliced the loaf for her mother's toast. "Couldn't you just try to ignore it?"

"I don't think I can do that any longer. It's making both of us miserable. Look how you've just made a special trip to the supermarket for her bread. It isn't as if it's a dietary requirement."

"I do it to keep the peace, Kev."

"Well you shouldn't have to. We're all adults here. We should be able to sort it out." He slumped onto a kitchen chair and grimaced. His thoughts were racing. He heard the upstairs bathroom door close and knew their conversation would have to end as soon as Shirley came down. But he didn't want to stop. He wanted to bring it to a head. "When was the last time we had a day to ourselves?"

Alison didn't answer. She bit at her lip. "You can't remember, can you?" Kevin said.

"What can't you remember?" Shirley said brightly as she came into the kitchen. "Ah, my favourite toast. What can't you remember?"

Kevin saw his wife open her mouth to answer and knew she was about to invent something to cover up the true content of their conversation.

"Here we are, Shirley," he said with forced enthusiasm. "Breakfast's ready. A bit late but better late than never, eh? We were just saying how it's time we had a day out somewhere nice."

"Oh, lovely," Shirley said. "Where were you thinking of?"

Kevin saw Alison cringe.

"We haven't decided yet," he said.

Shirley said, "There's an open garden day around the villages a week tomorrow. That would be nice. It's always interesting to see how other people organise their planting. It might give you some ideas, Kevin."

'Well, there you are, then," Kevin said. "You go to your open gardens day, Shirley. Alison and I would like to have a day to ourselves."

He waited for the fallout. Alison kept her head down and chewed silently. Shirley pushed her plate away and leaned back in her chair.

"Far be it from me to criticise . . ." she said.

"Good! I knew you'd understand, Shirley. I want to take my wife out. It's a long time since we had a day together. Where would you like to go, darling?"

He stared at Alison, willing her to say the right thing.

"Oh, well," she said. "I'll have to think about it. You won't mind if Kev and I have a day out on our own, will you, Mum?"

"Why would I mind?" Shirley said. "Far be it from me to point out that . . ."

"Good," Kevin interrupted his mother-in-law again. "We knew you'd understand, didn't we Ally?"

Shirley scraped back her chair. Slowly she left the table and went upstairs to her room. On her breakfast plate lay her two slices of nutty wholemeal toast untouched.

"Don't even think about going after her," Kevin said.

"But we've upset her. I should go and see if she's all right."

"She's perfectly fine. Alison, your mother is not ill. She's bloody marvellous for her age. Strong as an ox. We've only got ourselves to blame for what's happened since she came to us. We've let it happen."

"I couldn't see her struggling on her own after Dad died."

"Yes, I know. I'd want to do the same for my own parents if they were still here. You know I've always been in agreement Shirley should come to us. But it's gone too far, sweetheart. I don't like the way she's taking over our lives. It's got to stop and I need you to be with me on this."

He scrutinised Alison's face for signs of doubt. Her brow was knitted.

"I don't know," she said. "She sometimes makes me feel so guilty."

"I'm going to deal with this. Right now."

"What are you going to do?"

"I'm taking over." He made for the door.

"Oh, please be kind," Alison called after him.

Shirley was sitting on her bed. Kevin sat beside her and waited for her to speak first.

"You don't want me here with you, Kevin, do you?" she said.

"Is that what you really think? That must make you feel awful."

"It does."

"Well, it isn't true. We want everything to work out for all of us. That means sometimes Alison and I want to do things as a couple."

Shirley squirmed and began kneading her fingers. Quietly she said, "I get lonely."

Kevin knew how much it had taken for his mother-in-law to admit to that. He took her hands in his.

"We'll always be here for you, Shirley," he said. "You have a home here with us forever and we want everybody to be happy. Will you have a chat with Alison and come up with some ideas how we can improve our time together?"

He knew he'd have to take the helm again from time to time but felt he'd made a step in the right direction.

Spider Baby

It's spider season. Every year, right about now, thousands of the godless eight-legged bastards emerge from the bowels of hell (or the garden, whichever's nearest) with the sole intention of tormenting humankind.
Charlie Brooker 1971 -

He is tall and very thin and pale. Mary has never spoken her nickname for him. His father, God rest, wouldn't have appreciated the fact she thought of her stepson as *Spider Baby*. Like the old film. But not funny.

She's never felt like his stepmother and the boy has never treated her as one. He's been locked in his own interests since Mary has known him, an awkward child, clinging to his father, afraid of the world and most things in it.

Spider Baby didn't have conversations. He talked *at* people, telling them his favourite subjects *ad nauseum:* television schedules, bus timetables, route maps and road numbers. He could recite flight plans for every European airline and tell you how they'd changed from the previous year. He talked to take control. He had no idea how boring he was.

When he was fourteen and stayed in his room longer than ever, growing taller and thinner and paler up there in the dark, black hair sprouted on his upper lip and on his long, thin arms and long, thin legs. He developed an odd gait, stooped at the shoulders with his spidery hair-covered hands flexed in front of him and his long thin fingers dripping as if he were sitting at an invisible piano. Or his game console. He talked about *League of Legends* and *World of Warcraft* and how he was going to build his own server and over clock his water-cooled processor. He ate *gamers'* food: pizza and toasted sandwiches, things made quickly that he could eat with one hand while operating the console with the other.

His father used to say it was just a phase. Best to ignore it. Let him get on with it. There were worse things the boy could do.

Spider Baby is twenty-five now. He spends all his time gaming. He hardly talks to Mary at all. There would be no point in talking, he says. She wouldn't understand any of it. Why waste his time? He still eats gamers' food and drinks from cans or Java. He descends from his lair only when he's hungry. It makes her shudder to see him creep about the house with his bent back and long hairy Spider Hands.

With her good arm she wheels her chair to the window of their ground floor flat and looks out at the car by the kerb. There's still a small dent where Spider Baby hit her before he reversed over her legs. He said it was an accident.

She depends on Spider Baby now. If only his father hadn't always done everything for him. If only he hadn't babied him. Given in to him all the time. There'd be something other than a lecture about *Call of Duty* and cheese on toast for lunch served by Spider Fingers.

A Practical Woman

Dream in a pragmatic way
Aldous Huxley 1894-1963

The cutting from the tidal river ran right up beside the cottage. Sylvia stood on the decking out front with her coffee and took in her surroundings: Norfolk in winter. Above, pale blue sky streaked with filmy clouds stretched lazily beyond reeds and a stand of scrubby trees on the far bank of the river. The tide was changing: water lapped at the hulls of boats moored along the cutting; halyards slapped at masts with a tinkling sound.

A haven of peace. An escape from everyday life. A sanctuary. A solitary cup of coffee while she attempted to clear her mind.

He would love this place, she thought. *He would love to be beside the water surrounded by nature like this.*

And therein lay the reason she'd rented the holiday cottage for a week alone. The midwinter off-season ensured there was hardly another soul to be seen.

Soul: a word she'd paid little attention to throughout her life, not least the question of her own soul, her own deepest feelings and needs. Life always got in the way, didn't it? There was always work, always so much to be done it left little time to consider one's spiritual wellbeing. Now that retirement beckoned she'd have all the time in the world for things that brought her pleasure, satisfied her yearnings. Wouldn't she?

"I think it's wonderful you've met someone, Mum. When can I meet him?" her daughter Libby had said when she'd first mentioned Gordon by name one Sunday lunchtime. "Tell me all about him. Come on."

Sylvia hadn't known where to begin. Truth be told, she hadn't expected any new beginnings that included a man. She'd contemplated a house move: a sensible downsizing to reduce bills; perhaps joining one of those scholarly-type trips abroad to learn about other cultures. India, maybe. New Zealand even, to see where they'd filmed *Lord Of The Rings*. In her imaginings she'd always travelled alone. Her plans for the rest of her life included her daughter and grandchildren. But a man?

Gordon had been such a lovely surprise. Comfortable with one another from the outset they had fallen into an easy friendship with a remarkably similar sense of humour and a shared love of music. And how they'd talked! They could talk about anything and everything with openness and true sincerity.

"He sounds just right for you, Mum," Libby had said. "What are you worrying about?"

"Am I worrying?"

"Yes. Look at you. Your eyes are all screwed up and your mouth is doing that thing you used to do when I was a girl in trouble for being naughty."

"I'm not doing that. Am I?"

"Mum. Give him a chance. What have you got to lose?"

A heron swooped past and landed on a nearby tree stump. With his neck arched like a question mark, his head lowered, he scrutinised the dyke below him with yellow eyes sharp as pins and burning with intent.

Sylvia watched and waited. She didn't take risks. It simply wasn't in her nature. Like the heron, there had to be a good reason for whatever she did. A single parent since her thirties, she was always careful, determinedly making plans and seeing them through. She'd lived a life not without its ups and downs but in the knowledge she'd be able to cope with whatever fate sent her way.

Gordon was offering a different kind of future from the one she'd imagined. A spiritual man, happiest working outdoors, a lover of animals and his young grandchildren he was comfortable in his skin. He was able to articulate his emotions. He had an easy-going nature fluid as the water in the cutting, able to flow this way and that. He was like no other man she'd ever known.

Her confidence faltered. Fleetingly she wondered whether she would be enough.

In a flash of white and with a splash of silver the heron made his strike.

There now, she thought as the heron flew off. *He got what he came here for. But what if he'd missed his lunch target?*

She laughed aloud as the answer burst into her thoughts. Energy fizzed through her limbs and fired her nervous system. Warmth pulsed in her veins. Confidence restored, she recognised her body's reactions as a sense of sheer joy. All anxiety fell away as she understood the reality of her new way of thinking. It was simple! Even if he'd failed to catch his meal, the heron would still be a heron. He wouldn't worry about failing the next time. He wouldn't be afraid of trying again. Surely his very existence depended on him being himself, doing his heron thing fishing for his sustenance, taking the risk of a possible further loss?

She brought her cup to her lips. Her coffee had gone cold. No matter. She'd make another but she had a call to make first. Sometimes you had to take risks.

She went indoors to get her phone. The drive would take him four hours. It would be dark by the time he arrived. Tomorrow they would stand together to face the future and watch the tide change.

ABOUT THE AUTHOR

Celia Micklefield has worked in an accountant's office, a high street retail store, a textile mill and a shoe factory as well as short stints in a fish and chip shop, behind the bar in a pub and running a slimming club. She studied for a teaching degree and went into teaching at high school, became a partner in an import and wholesale business and ran a craft outlet at a country shopping experience. She returned to teaching where her last position was at a sixth form college.

She was born in West Yorkshire and has lived in Aberdeenshire and the south of France. She currently lives in Norfolk.

More books by Celia Micklefield:

Patterns of our Lives

Trobairitz- the Storyteller

Trobairitz - her story continues

The Sandman and Mrs Carter

A Measured Man

Rosie, John and the God of Putting Things Right

American Tan short stories

Arse(d) Ends short stories

People Who Hurt non fiction

All available in Paperback and for Kindle. Visit Amazon's Celia Micklefield page.
You can subscribe to Celia's Random Thoughts blog on her website
www.celiamicklefield.com

She has a Facebook author page and is on X (Twitter) @cmicklefield

Printed in Great Britain
by Amazon